D0200465

STEPHANIE S. TOLAN

WHO'S THERE?

MORROW JUNIOR BOOKS
NEW YORK

Library of Congress Cataloging-in-Publication Data
Tolan, Stephanie S.   Who's there?/Stephanie S. Tolan   p.   cm.
Summary: When fourteen-year-old Drew and her mute younger
brother come to live with their father's estranged relatives after
their parents' sudden death, they discover that the house
is haunted by ghosts and a deadly family secret.
ISBN 0-688-04611-8
[1. Grief—Fiction.   2. Ghosts—Fiction.   3. Brothers and sisters—Fiction.
4. Mutism, Elective—Fiction.]   I. Title.   PZ7.T5735Wh   1994
[Fic]—dc20   94-15384   CIP   AC

For Marlene Sandler—
to whom nothing is strange—
with thanks from the child
who found a voice.

CHAPTER
ONE

DREW BRODERICK STARED hard out the car window at the green rolling hills of New York, the dark blue of distant mountains behind. Suddenly, she was blinking back tears. She turned in the seat until her back was to Evan and rubbed one hand across her eyes fast. She would not cry! The Tildens had not seen her cry, not once since that first awful afternoon, that hysterical night. Not once since then. Evan had his silence and she had her own rock-hard resolve.

So why had the world blurred suddenly, and the fist clenched without warning in her chest now? All the daily reminders of loss had been left behind in Massachusetts, and she would never have to pass the blackened ruins, the scorched and mutilated maple tree again.

The dream. The memory washed over her now, as if her mind was only just catching up to her feelings. It was that dream coming back to her, the one that had wakened her this morning in the chill before dawn. She'd found herself sitting bolt upright, her quilt in a tangle, her heart pounding. There'd been tears on her cheeks then, too, and she'd hastily scrubbed them away with the hem of the sheet for fear Tillie would see. Tillie was still asleep, though, her breath moving noisily in and out of her open mouth.

Drew had sat very still then, waiting for her heart to calm, feeling as if she were tangled, too, in the tattered edges of the dream. Fear. No—terror. Someone—something—chasing her. Herself running, but more and more slowly, her feet mired in something sticky, something heavy. The thing behind her closing in. And Evan there, too, Evan and herself and evil...

Now, in the car, she tried to push the memory away. It was nothing—an ordinary nightmare. Probably number Fifteen B in the psychiatrist's book of standard dreams of traumatized children.

Traumatized adolescents, she corrected herself—she'd turned fourteen now, not a child anymore. Dr. Rosenberry would recognize the dream immediately, show her on the page: *Nightmare Fifteen B—Unknown monster chasing, feet unable to run, monster gaining—subject wakes up in tears of terror.* No matter how carefully you closed everything off while you were awake, dreams could betray you, could flood you with feelings when your defenses were down. Dr. Rosenberry had talked a lot about dreams.

This one had to do with last fall, not with this trip, this change, this beginning. But still the shreds of fear clung, as if the dream was not behind her, safely past, but ahead. Her heart was beating hard and fast again.

Drew blinked and took a deep, slow breath. Ridiculous, she told herself, and tried to pull the cloak of numbness around herself again. No feelings, none. That was how she'd managed so far and how she would keep managing. She settled back in the seat, bumping her elbow on Pandora's travel case.

Pandora shifted slightly inside but did not complain. She had never been one of those car-hating cats. Pandora the quiet, the calm and sedate. Pandora, Evan's white shadow.

"Almost there," Professor Tilden said, drumming his hands on the steering wheel. "Just passed a sign that said five miles to Riverton. According to the map your aunt sent, Rose Hill is just this side of town, off a road that runs along the river."

"Tillie's so sorry she couldn't miss her gymkhana to come along," Mrs. Tilden said for the third time that day. "She'd love to see your new ho— ah, Rose Hill," she corrected quickly.

Home, she was going to say, Drew thought. She changed the word in case things don't work out. Everybody—the Tildens, Dr. Rosenberry, the people at the college—everybody was determined to offer alternative plans in case this whole idea was a disaster. But it *would* work out. Drew knew it would. It had to, because no matter what people said, there was nowhere else for them to go. Rose Hill had to be their home.

And why not? They had family there, after all. Their parents hadn't left a will to say what was to become of them, and the Tildens had taken them in so they'd both be able to stay in school, have the same friends. But it hadn't ever, not for a moment, felt like family, or home. Drew focused on the edge of the road rushing past and remembered the day Professor Tilden told her that he'd found her father's family, a family she had never known about: an aunt and a grand-father, living in a house large enough to have a name, not just an address. Rose Hill, Riverton, New York. The Brodericks of Rose Hill meant a placc to bclong again and bc safc.

"You okay, Evan? Not carsick or anything?" Mrs. Tilden asked without turning to look at him, as if he might actually answer her.

Evan, his small fine-boned hand clutching the handle of Pandora's case, shook his head solemnly, a movement Mrs. Tilden could not see. It doesn't matter, Drew thought. She doesn't need an answer, because the question wasn't real. It was just another attempt to get Evan to speak—a trick—as if he might forget his silence if the question was routine enough and if she seemed to expect him to answer in words. Dr. Rosenberry must have told them to do it; they did it so often. "Where are you going, Evan?" "When did you let Pandora out, Evan?" "Pan-cakes or waffles, Evan?"

He's not stupid, Drew thought, as she did every time. Did they really think after all these months he'd slip, that he might just say "Waffles" one morning as if he was some ordinary hungry eight-year-old kid? She looked at him now, his pale legs sticking out from his shorts, his knees small and knobby. Just Evan. Just the same as ever, his light brown hair curling slightly at his ears and over his forehead, his elfish pointy chin, his huge brown eyes seeming to stare at the back of the seat in front of him, their lids half-closed. Except that for nearly eight months he had not said a single word—not at school, not with his friends, not with Drew.

She tried to guess what he was thinking as Rose Hill got closer and everything they knew farther away. It was no good. She might as well ask what Pandora thought. On October fourteenth, her brother, Evan, like so much else in her life, had become an impenetrable mystery.

Drew forced herself to smile. Dr. Rosenberry had told her that putting a smile on your face automatically lightened your mood. Scientific fact. And she'd been right. It was the best tool Drew had. She felt her cheeks get rounder with the smile, her heart lighter, and she closed her eyes to imagine Rose Hill once more. For weeks she'd been doing it, and the pictures came easily now. Home. A big, welcoming white house with a broad, columned front porch; a swing, painted dark green; and flower boxes at the windows. Aunt Jocelyn, a lively woman with pink cheeks and a rounded, comfortable body in a flowered dress and ruffled apron. Grandfather Broderick—Grandpa—white-haired, slightly stooped, with a flowing mustache. Both hurrying down the porch steps to welcome their long-lost family. In her imagining, she carefully avoided the question she couldn't answer—how she and Evan had gotten lost in the first place.

The car was slowing, turning. Drew opened her eyes. "Watch carefully," Professor Tilden said. "It should be a driveway on the right side of the road, not too much farther. According to the map, there'll be a sign."

Drew leaned forward and peered ahead and to the right. Evan was looking now, too. Trees, bushes, telephone poles, a sense of looming green as hills rose behind. The car was slowing as all four of them looked for the sign. Drew discovered she was holding her breath. And then a whoosh of air through nose and mouth. "There it is!" she said. "There!"

It was much more than she'd imagined.

Two huge redbrick gateposts supported black wrought-iron gates angled back on either side of a wide, smooth drive between the trees. A tall black iron fence stretched away on either side. On top of the gateposts, two stone Oriental dogs faced each other with wide, smiling faces, tails curled tightly over their backs, each with one front paw on a stone ball. Carved into stone tablets set into the brick on either side was *Rose Hill* and under that *1810*.

"Wow," Drew breathed. "Wow!"

"I'll say." Professor Tilden turned between the gates and inched forward. The drive curved to the left and headed upward among the trees, then curved right. Drew could see nothing but the trees and the drive until they suddenly pulled out of the trees and the house lay ahead, atop a vast sloping lawn, flanked by two enormous oak trees. Drew gasped. Not the white frame house of her imagining, Rose Hill was the dark red brick of the gateposts. Enormous, Drew thought. And then, Beautiful.

Professor Tilden whistled. "Georgian," he said. "Pure Georgian!"

How could she not have known this house all her life? Drew wondered. How could their father ever have left it?

The driveway split, one side going around the house to the right, toward separate buildings behind, the other curving in a circle in front and coming back to itself. Professor Tilden followed the curve to the left and pulled to a stop in front of the stone steps that led up to a wide dark green door in the center of the house. No porch, Drew thought. Tall windows, though, their sparkling rectangular panes trimmed in white, green shutters open against the brick. White curtains inside, pulled back. Beautiful, Drew thought again. And then she looked up. The windows of the second floor, beneath the peaked slate roof, were blank, blinds pulled down—like closed eyes, blank and still.

No one was hurrying to greet them. The green door remained shut. Professor Tilden turned off the car's engine. "Guess we need to ring the bell," he said, "let them know we're here." Drew stayed where she was, staring up at the flat, blank windows of the second floor. Had she noticed a movement there somewhere? If so, it was gone.

Mrs. Tilden got out of the car and opened Evan's door. Eyes wide now, taking in the expanse of house, Evan stepped out into the sunlight. He stood for a moment, looking upward, then turned back for Pandora's case. As he brought it out, a deep, piercing yowl erupted from inside. It rose in pitch and tone until Drew seemed to feel it on the inside of her skull. It seemed to bounce back at them from the closed front of the house. Evan put a finger through an air hole and the sound trailed off into a deep, throaty, snarling growl. No one moved in the welcome stillness.

"Well...," Mrs. Tilden said at last. "Well...what do you suppose...?"

Drew, a chill at the base of her neck, pulled herself out of the car into the warm June sun. The green door opened.

CHAPTER

LIKE THE HOUSE, the woman who came through the door was entirely different from Drew's imagining. She was tall and broad-shouldered but slightly stooped. Though it was not yet noon, she looked worn, as if she was at the end of a long day of exhausting work. She wore heavy sandals, blue jeans, and a long-sleeved plaid shirt, its cuffs rolled up. Drew took that in and then looked at the woman's face and blinked. And blinked again.

She had somehow forgotten, creating her mental pictures, this aunt's relationship to her father. But now it was impossible to miss. The high, broad forehead, squarish jaw, short, straight nose. It was as if a sculptor had made a woman's figure and then put on it her father's face, only thinning it a little and adding longer hair, pulled back at the base of the neck instead of shaggy around the ears. All the family photographs had been lost in the fire; Drew had not seen her father's image in all this time. But here it was, alive, three-dimensional, on the body of a stranger. Not a stranger, she amended—her father's younger sister, her aunt.

"Sorry I didn't hear you drive up," the woman was saying. "I was with Father." She came down the steps, her right hand held out to the Tildens. "Professor and Mrs. Tilden, I'm Jocelyn Broderick." When they had shaken hands, a bit stiffly, she turned to the children. "Aunt Jocelyn to you, I suppose." Drew felt frozen as those half-familiar eyes held hers, then turned to Evan. For a long moment the woman stared at him as if she was looking for something in his face, something she did not find. Evan looked down at Pandora's case, clutched against his chest. At last she smiled, and Drew thought the expression looked awkward, as if hers was a face not used to smiling. "Evan. And Drew, of course. And who is in there?"

She gestured toward the case. Inside, Pandora was quiet. Whatever had caused her to make such a dreadful sound, she was apparently over it. "Pandora," Drew answered. "Evan's cat."

"Ah yes, Pandora. She'll be the first cat Rose Hill has had intentionally in a generation. There are strays we feed sometimes...in the carriage house. Welcome."

The woman did not offer to shake hands with her or even touch the top of Evan's head, as adults seemed almost magnetically drawn to do. For a moment, Drew was disappointed. She had imagined hugs. Then she thought it was probably better this way. Hugs this soon couldn't possibly mean anything. All that counted was that Aunt Jocelyn was family and Rose Hill was home.

Professor Tilden had the back of the car up and was removing luggage. "Bring the children's things in," Aunt Jocelyn said. "Lunch is ready. I understand you need to get back on the road."

"Yes, we're sorry to have to rush," Mrs. Tilden said, picking up one of Evan's bags. "Our daughter's riding with her stable's team in a gymkhana near Williamstown today, and we're picking her up on the way back. We'd have taken more time for all of this, but we leave for London on

Monday. Things are unbelievably hectic...."

She's nervous, Drew thought, picking up her duffel bag and following Aunt Jocelyn, Mrs. Tilden, still talking, and Evan up the stone steps. Surely she'd already explained all of that in letters and phone calls.

Professor Tilden came behind with the rest of the luggage, two medium-sized canvas suitcases. Not much, Drew thought, considering it was all she and Evan had in the world. Except for her backpack and the clothes they'd worn to school October fourteenth, everything they owned was new.

All we have in the world, she thought as she reached the open door, and us, coming home. She started to arrange a smile on her face, but before she had it in place, it had become real. Inside, the front hall was bathed in sunshine that streamed through the tall windows across the patterns of a deep red Oriental rug. A long, steep stairway rose almost in front of them, the matching runner held in place at each step with a brass rod, a gleaming wood banister rising with the stairs, supported by intricately carved spindles. Above, from the center of a white medallion in the ceiling, hung a crystal chandelier with tiers of glittering pendants that made rainbows on the pale gold-and-white-striped walls. "Oooh," she heard herself say. Whatever uneasiness had stirred as she looked up at the blank windows of the second floor disappeared. This is the most beautiful house in the whole world, Drew thought.

She didn't change her mind when, after they'd left the luggage at the base of the stairs, Jocelyn Broderick led them to the left and through a room lined from floor to ceiling with glass-fronted bookshelves, then through a dining room with another chandelier in the center and smaller ones mounted on the walls, to a huge kitchen. On the far wall of the kitchen was a fireplace Evan could have walked into without ducking, its hearth made of rough stone. The cabinets, between tall uncurtained windows, were painted white above long counters of yellow ceramic tile. In the center of the room was a round table covered with a yellow-and-white-checked cloth. Five places were set with heavy plates and silverware, cobalt blue glasses, and yellow napkins.

"I hope you all eat tuna salad," Aunt Jocelyn said, taking a blue bowl out of a refrigerator that looked big enough for a restaurant. "Put Pandora's case down and let her out," she told Evan. "She can explore while we eat. Is she an indoor or an outdoor cat?"

Evan nodded, and Aunt Jocelyn smiled, more easily this time, Drew thought. "Both, eh?" Evan nodded again. "We'd better keep her inside till she's used to being here. We wouldn't want her to get lost. I assume you brought a litter box?"

Evan nodded.

"Better get it. We'll put it in the back pantry." When Evan had set Pandora's case carefully on the hearth and gone back for the litter box, Aunt Jocelyn turned to the Tildens. "He does all right without words, doesn't he?"

Professor Tilden nodded, but Mrs. Tilden jumped in before he could say anything. "Dr. Rosenberry, you know, the therapist who's been working with him—"

Aunt Jocelyn nodded. "I've spoken to her."

"Yes, well, she says it doesn't matter how well he communicates; it's important that he begin *talking* again as soon as possible. She'd thought keeping him with his friends would help, but it didn't. They knew him well enough that he was able to communicate whatever he needed to—or wanted to. Most of the time, he just isolated himself from other children, even his best friends. It was a long school year. Dr. Rosenberry says he won't begin to heal till he begins to talk. As I told you, she thinks being in a new place where there aren't so many reminders will help. New place and new people. We've tried and tried to get him to talk, but—"

"Grief's an individual thing," Jocelyn Broderick said, waving Drew to a chair and indicating where the Tildens should sit. "Young or old, we cope the best we can. No one can say for anyone else how much time it takes."

The color rose in Mrs. Tilden's neck as she sat down and made a production of shaking out her napkin. When she'd settled it in her lap, she looked around at the four other chairs and place settings. "Won't Mr. Broderick be joining us?"

"My father does not leave his room. He's quite ill, as I told you. When he's able to eat some lunch, as he did today, he usually sleeps till late afternoon."

"I'm sorry," Mrs. Tilden said. "Douglas and Marianne were our closest friends. We would have liked to meet Douglas's father."

Professor Tilden chuckled as he sat down

next to his wife. "Not that we ever knew he had a father. Or any family at all, for that matter. Douglas was always something of a mystery man. For all we knew, he simply materialized on campus fourteen years ago, fully grown, with a Ph.D. in classics, a lovely young wife, and a new baby."

In the silence after these words, Drew smoothed the napkin carefully on her lap, concentrating on the weave of the cloth. At the mention of her parents, images had started to appear in her mind. She forced them away. The Tildens never mentioned Douglas and Marianne Broderick in front of Evan. They were afraid of reminding him, starting him crying as he had cried those first awful weeks. They were never so careful about her.

"Something of a mystery man," Professor Tilden said again.

Jocelyn Broderick brought a large pitcher to the table. "Lemonade?" Drew nodded, looking away from the face that was so like her father's. She wondered if her aunt would explain, now, why none of them had ever heard of the Brodericks of Rose Hill. Her father had referred to himself and their mother as "orphans of the storm," and everyone thought it was as literally true for him as it was for her. When she was little, Drew had sometimes asked about his mother and father. He would only shake his head. "Long gone," he would say. "Long, long gone." What had happened to send him away from Rose Hill? To keep him from telling them about their grandfather, their aunt?

No explanation came. "Lemonade?" Jocelyn asked the Tildens.

When Evan came back, lunch waited while the litter box was put away and Evan raised the lid of Pandora's carrying case. Drew watched as the thin white cat stepped out and began to move around the kitchen, her tail high. Now, she seemed only curious, looking and sniffing. She made no sound. Drew felt herself relaxing, as if she'd been tensed for a blow that hadn't come.

"Leave her to it. She can't get anyplace she shouldn't be," Jocelyn said, pulling Evan's chair out for him. "You do eat tuna, don't you?"

Evan nodded.

"He eats everything," Mrs. Tilden said. "Except turnips."

"Don't blame you," Jocelyn said, looking solemnly into Evan's eyes. "Disgusting vegetable. Second only to okra."

Evan grinned. For just a moment, the pixie

look that had once been Evan's trademark had appeared. There and gone. But unmistakable. As if something that had been very long asleep behind his eyes had wakened for just a moment and peeked out. Drew saw the Tildens exchange glances.

When lunch was finished, Mrs. Tilden offered to help clear up the dishes, but Jocelyn shook her head. "You should be getting on the road if you expect to get home at a decent hour. Is Williamstown far out of your way?"

"Not very," Professor Tilden said. "It'll add about an hour."

Outside a few minutes later, Drew shook hands with Professor Tilden and watched as he and Mrs. Tilden each hugged Evan. Mrs. Tilden's cheeks were wet as she came to hug Drew. "Remember now, honey, we'll be back the last week in August." She glanced over her shoulder at Jocelyn Broderick and whispered into Drew's ear, "If this doesn't work out, you're welcome to come back to us. Tillie has loved having a sister and brother this year."

Tillie doesn't have a sister and brother, Drew thought as she accepted Mrs. Tilden's hug, feeling the tight blond curls against her cheek. But she nodded.

Mrs. Tilden spoke again in her normal voice. "We'll send postcards and let you know addresses so you can write. You be sure and let us know if"—her eyes flicked toward Evan and back—"you know, if anything changes."

Drew put a smile in place as the Tildens got into their car and held it there carefully as the car moved away. Mrs. Tilden waved steadily all the way around the circle and down the long drive toward the road.

Before the car had disappeared around the first curve, Evan had gone back inside. Probably to find Pandora, Drew thought.

Jocelyn Broderick puffed out her cheeks and let the air out in a rush. "So," she said. "Here we are."

"Yes," Drew said. She looked down the long slope of lawn to the trees, then off to the distant blue of mountains and felt her shoulders lift, as if they'd been supporting a heavy weight that had been suddenly removed. "Here we are."

CHAPTER

THREE

"THIS HOUSE IS far too big for two people," Jocelyn said as she led Drew and Evan, with Pandora following, up the stairs. "So we keep the second floor closed off. No one's lived up here for more than thirty years. I've cleaned, of course, but I'm afraid it's still a little musty and dusty."

The walls were covered with the same gold-and-white-striped paper as the downstairs hall, but here it did not seem as light and welcoming. As they reached the top of the stairs, Drew turned to look behind her toward the front of the house. The doors to the rooms above the living room, hall, and library were closed, so the only light in the upper hall came from two white-globed ceiling lights. As bright as the downstairs of Rose Hill was with the afternoon sun streaming through tall windows, the upstairs was a sort of dim twilight. It was cooler up here, Drew thought, almost chilly.

The red Oriental runner from the stairs ran the length of a hall that led directly away from the stairway, with polished wood floors showing on either side. The doors along the hall were closed, too.

"I've put you in what's called the 'new house,'" Jocelyn explained. "It was added in 1894. The 'old house' is Georgian, just one big rectangle, symmetrical inside and out. When they needed more room, they decided to build straight back from the center of the original to keep from changing the look of the house from the front." She opened the first door on the left. "This will be your room, Evan." She switched on the overhead light.

The room had clearly been a child's room, its walls blue, with a border of jungle animals around the ceiling. Matching jungle-animal curtains hung at the tall window, and a low chest,

topped with a cushion covered in the same fabric, was set like a window seat against the sill.
The twin bed, a dresser, a bookcase, and a rocking chair were all made of bamboo and rattan,
and a worn quilt covered the bed, a golden-eyed
lion face in its center.

"We've kept the shades pulled down to keep
the sun from fading everything," Jocelyn said,
"but you'll want a little light. These windows get
the afternoon sun, so it'll be hot in here on a July
afternoon." She raised the shade halfway up and
sunlight streamed in. Evan put his bag down and
stood gravely in the center of the room, looking
at the framed pictures of lions and tigers hanging
on the walls.

As he looked at the pictures, Aunt Jocelyn
looked at him intently. As if she was trying to see
right through him, Drew thought. Was it just that
he didn't talk, she wondered, that made Evan so
special? Or was it something else? "You won't be
bothered by those, will you?" Jocelyn asked him.
"They won't give you nightmares or anything?"

Evan shook his head. He lifted one hand and
gently touched the elephant lamp on the dresser.

"I'd have liked to spruce these rooms up a little—redecorate and make them a bit more mod-

ern. But Father's too ill to have workmen in and out...."

Pandora leapt lightly onto the cushion at the window and settled herself in the sunlight, her front paws together, her body carefully symmetrical. In moments, her purr could be heard across the room. "She seems comfortable enough, anyway."

Evan nodded, his lips tilted toward the beginning of a smile. Drew wondered who had lived in this room, who had chosen the jungle theme.

"Your room is down the hall and on the other side," Jocelyn told her, turning to go into the hall. Drew followed her out. "It used to be mine."

Drew smiled again as she went into the room her aunt had entered. Soft light from two milk-glass lamps on a white dressing table lit the pale lavender walls of a room decorated with violets. At the tall windows, violet print curtains were tied back with purple ribbons. Here, too, the blinds were pulled down. Jocelyn raised them halfway, and daylight gave the lavender walls a touch of warmer pink.

"I'm glad you didn't change this room," Drew said. "I like it."

Watercolor paintings on heavy paper hung

on every wall. Rose Hill was the subject of several of them, painted in different seasons and from different angles. In one, the center of the circular drive was filled with rosebushes, blooming in a profusion of pinks and reds, yellows and whites. The colors in all the paintings were vivid and clear, the light seeming as real as if it came out of the paper itself.

"They're beautiful," Drew said. She noticed the initials J.B. at the corner of each one. "Did you do them?"

Her aunt nodded. "A very long time ago." She pointed to a door opposite the twin beds. "The closet's there; you can leave your suitcase on the shelf when you've unpacked. Towels and washcloths are in the bathroom, the next door down on this side. The back stairs are at the end of the hall. They lead down to the pantry off the kitchen." She paused, glanced around the room, and made a helpless gesture with both hands. "I hope the two of you won't be unbearably bored here. I'm afraid I don't have time to organize much activity for you. We're pretty far from town and there aren't any kids close for the two of you to spend time with."

"That's okay," Drew said. "We'll be all right."

She didn't want to meet other kids yet, to have to start in with the inevitable explanations.

Jocelyn went out into the hall and then came back to the doorway. "Father will be awake shortly. He wants to meet you both. In the meantime, you can unpack. I'll let you know when he's ready to see you. I should warn you not to expect too much from your grandfather. He's very old and very sick." And she was gone. Drew, still holding her duffel bag, stood for a moment, marveling at the watercolors her aunt had so abruptly dismissed.

Then she put her duffel on the nearest bed and went back to get her other bag. She paused at the top of the stairway a moment before going down, looking across the wide, dim hall past the railing that guarded the stairwell to the three closed doors across the front of the house. Who had lived in those rooms, or the two others on either side of the stairwell?

The hall where her room and Evan's room were, the new house, now held daylight; from their open doors, light spilled across the red rug. But the old house was as dark and blank as it had seemed from outside when she looked up at its blind windows from the car. She remembered the sense she'd had that something had moved up here. She'd been mistaken—that was obvious. It had been thirty years since these rooms had been lived in. Thirty years of quiet, of closed doors and drawn shades.

She shook away the feeling those doors gave her and hurried downstairs. It was just as Jocelyn had said: Two people didn't need all the space of this house. Couldn't use it. But now she and Evan would bring life and light to the upstairs. They would open doors and windows, blow away a generation of dust. She and Evan would unpack in rooms that were to be their own rooms, and then they would be settled—at home. This was a place she wanted to stay. Beautiful, safe. She wouldn't be alone in the world anymore. She would belong again—to the Brodericks of Rose Hill.

She found Evan sitting next to Pandora on the window seat, looking out over a long grassy slope toward a stretch of woods. "Here's your other bag. Aunt Jocelyn says to unpack and then we're going to meet...Grandfather." It seemed strange to use that word for a person she'd never even seen. She looked out over the scene Evan was gazing at. "Some backyard." Evan turned to her for a moment and nodded, then turned back to the window, one hand resting lightly on Pandora's back.

"Get your things unpacked so we'll be ready when Aunt Jocelyn calls us down." Evan nodded again.

Drew hurriedly unpacked her own clothes and put her books and notebooks on the desk. She deliberated for a moment or two and then chose the bed nearest the window and set the stuffed unicorn Tillie Tilden had given her for her fourteenth birthday in the center of the pillow. She didn't like the unicorn, with its slick rainbow-hued bow and fat plush horn. She hadn't even named it. What should have been leaning against that pillow was Charley, her old, tattered teddy bear. But Charley was gone, along with everything else. Might as well never have been, she reminded herself, so no point in thinking about him. The nameless unicorn was what she had now. Now was all that counted. At least the unicorn made the room look more lived in.

When she was done, Aunt Jocelyn had not yet called them down. So she ventured down the hallway and found the black-and-white-tiled bathroom with the old-fashioned footed tub.

Still Aunt Jocelyn had not called for them. Drew stood for a moment in the hall outside the bathroom. To her right were the back stairs; ahead, another closed door. After a moment, she stepped across and tried the knob. The door creaked open, revealing dusty gray-painted steps leading upward. There was a light switch with two buttons on the wall, one in and one out. She pushed the one that stuck out, and, as they reversed, a pale light went on overhead.

Hesitantly, Drew ventured up five steps to the landing, then the five more in the other direction. As she went up, it got warmer and warmer. She found herself in a huge, dim attic under the sloping roof of the new house, the only light coming from the bulb overhead and from what seemed to be low windows at either end of the old house. The hot, still air was full of the smell of dust and cobwebs, mildew and—she was sure— mouse dung.

Almost every inch of floor space was taken up with stacks of boxes, some closed and taped shut, some open or partly open, some with contents spilling out. Narrow pathways wound haphazardly between them. Behind boxes, she could make out the shapes of pieces of furniture, some of them nearly buried under boxes, as well. Just ahead, there was a massive dark red plush chair, its stuffing popping out in tufts, its seat occupied by a stack of shoe boxes and a battered Raggedy Ann doll with a dirty face and one arm missing.

With one finger, Drew lifted one of the cardboard flaps of a box near her. Inside were spiral notebooks and creased and crumpled notebook papers. The leftovers of a school year, probably. She closed it. She wished she had a flashlight. Beyond these boxes loomed mysterious shadowy shapes she longed to investigate. From the looks of it, the Brodericks must never have thrown anything away. Nearly two hundred years' worth of outgrown or broken or unwanted household items might be packed away under the sloping roofs—the whole history of a family she'd never known she had.

Reluctantly, she went back down the stairs. If Aunt Jocelyn said it was all right, she'd come back to explore.

She had just gotten to her room and was looking again at the watercolor with the rose garden in the center of the drive when Aunt Jocelyn called from the bottom of the back stairs. "Evan, Drew, Father is able to see you now."

CHAPTER
FOUR

AFTER THE BRIGHT hall, the room was so dark, it took time to adjust, to see more than vague shapes and shadows. Drew blinked. And the bulky darkness in front of her became a hospital bed, its head end raised, pillows lighter, the head against the pillows no more than a shadow. Jocelyn turned on a heavily shaded lamp on a table next to the bed and the shadow became a face.

If Aunt Jocelyn's face had seemed to be their father's but thinner, this face was their father's shrunken, dried, tanned like leather—like the mummy's face from the Egyptian section of her world history text. Wisps of white hair lay across a nearly bald, freckled skull. The eyes, above a narrow, bony nose, were closed. The jolly, rosy grandfather image Drew had built for herself dwindled and vanished. If the second floor felt chilly, this room, Drew noticed, was hot. Suffocating.

"Father," Aunt Jocelyn said. "The children are here."

Drew could feel Evan's presence almost directly behind her, as if he was using her as a shield.

"Father."

"I heard." A voice with the rasp of a file came from the thin lips. The eyelids opened and pale blue eyes seemed to focus with difficulty on Drew. "So, you're Douglas's children," the voice said. "Your name, girl?"

Drew swallowed. "Drew."

"That's it? Drew? What sort of a name is that?"

"My whole name is Drew Carolyn Broderick."

There was a long silence. Drew could hear the heavy tick of a clock from the shadows to her right and Evan's breathing behind her, as if he'd been running. "Carolyn Broderick was your grandmother," the voice said. "Did you know that?"

"No." Named for her grandmother. Why had she never known? "Dad never talked about his family."

"Nor his family about him." The old man turned his gaze on Jocelyn for a moment, then back. "Drew Carolyn. Your grandmother died of polio in 1958. Your father was sixteen. Old enough to get over it, one would have thought. But he never did."

Drew said nothing. *Old enough to get over it.* Like her.

A bony hand moved on the white coverlet, pointing. "And who is that behind you? Come out where I can see you, boy."

Evan moved slowly, his breath still audible, and stood beside her. She could feel him against her, quivering, like a frightened animal.

"Evan." The old man's brow furrowed and his pale eyes seemed darker suddenly. "Evan," he repeated, shaking his head, his hand still poised in the air, still pointing. His voice grew louder suddenly, as if he was angry. "You're nothing like him. Nothing at all!" Drew felt Evan turning to her as if for help, but she didn't know what to say or do. What did the old man mean? Was he crazy as well as sick? She touched Evan's hand.

"I understand you don't talk. That's good. I'm a sick man and I need quiet." Their grandfather lowered his hand but kept looking at Evan, measuring him, it seemed to Drew. Evan had taken his lower lip between his teeth, but he didn't look away. The clock ticked. Drew felt a trickle of perspiration run down her side.

"We didn't have to take you," the old man said finally, turning his eyes on Drew and leaning forward off his pillows with an effort. In the drawn face, his eyes were intense, and his voice, though raspy, was suddenly piercing. "I want you to know that we didn't have to take you. We're not legally responsible. Your father..." He paused, as if searching for words, then fell back. His hand twitched against the coverlet. "We didn't have to take you," he muttered, as if he'd exhausted his strength.

"We'll let you rest now, Father," Jocelyn said then. She moved between the old man and Evan and straightened his covers. "I'll be in with your medicine shortly."

She turned back to them and shooed them

toward the door. When they reached the hall, she closed the door carefully behind them, pulling on it until they'd all heard the latch click. "That's done," she said with a sigh. "I don't know about the two of you, but I could do with a brownie." She put her hand lightly on Evan's neck and headed him toward the kitchen. "There are all different kinds of medicine."

In the bright kitchen, so different from the dark, hot sickroom, Drew and Evan sat at the table while Jocelyn poured milk and set out a plateful of brownies. Evan stared down at his hands in his lap, unmoving, until she lifted his chin and offered to put a brownie into his mouth. He smiled then and took a bite. "Sorry about Father," she said to them both. "He's really quite ill. I'd like to tell you that he isn't himself because of it, but I'm not sure that's true. When he has the strength, he almost seems to enjoy being difficult. But you won't have to have much contact with him. He doesn't leave his room, and I can't think of many reasons for you to go there." She patted Evan's shoulder. "And don't worry about what he said about our not having to take you. We may not have much to offer, but you belong here. You're family."

"What did he mean that Evan wasn't anything like 'him'? Like who?" Drew asked. Evan nodded. It was a question he clearly wanted to have answered, too.

Aunt Jocelyn paused with her milk glass in the air and looked out the window. Drew began to think she wasn't going to answer. Finally, though, Jocelyn sighed. "Like the other Evan. My younger brother—your father's and mine. He died in the late summer of 1961, when he was only six." She turned to Evan. "You were named after him, apparently. As Drew was named for our mother."

It seemed that everywhere Drew went, everywhere she looked, she came somehow to death. "Was it polio?" she asked. "Did he get it, too?"

Jocelyn seemed startled. "Polio? Evan? Oh, no." She shook her head as if getting away from a swarm of gnats. "His death was an accident. Just an accident." She finished her milk and gathered up the glasses. "I'll put these dishes in the dishwasher, and the two of you can go off and do a little exploring. Stay where you can see the house and start getting to know Rose Hill. It's your home now, after all."

The word seemed to fold around Drew. In spite of the dark, hot room, the angry, raspy old man, this place was going to be home.

"Would it be okay if I explored the attic sometime?" Drew asked.

Jocelyn raised her eyebrows. "The attic? It's fine with me, but when you go, you'll probably wish you had a gas mask with you. Dust, cobwebs—it's a mess. And probably pretty warm."

Drew nodded. "That's okay. It looks like there's a lot of history up there."

"There's history up there, for sure. I don't think anyone has cleaned it out since the house was built." Jocelyn leaned against the counter and smiled. "When I was little, I used to play up there sometimes. And Douglas—your father—before me. It was crowded then, and a lot of junk's been added since. Mother used to say we should organize things, call the Historical Society to take anything valuable, and then just get rid of the rest. But it never happened, somehow. Things just kept being added and the old things shoved back. It'll be hard getting to anything really historical. That'll mostly be back under the eaves of the old house."

She opened a drawer in the cabinet next to her and rummaged for a moment, coming up, finally, with a battered flashlight. "When you go, you'll want to take this with you. There's no light in the part over the old house."

"Has the house been in your family—our family—from the beginning?" Drew asked.

"Heavens no! Father bought it in the early thirties. The owner had lost everything in the Depression and Father got it dirt cheap, as he used to say, at an auction. Antique roses and all."

Drew felt disappointment wash over her. She had hoped the attic would give her generations and generations of Brodericks. Distant, ancient, safe. "Antique roses?"

Jocelyn nodded. "The man Father bought it from was obsessed with them. He maintained gardens of the varieties that were planted when the house was first built and some that dated all the way back to the sixteenth century. For a while, Father paid someone to care for them, but it got to seem silly. Most of the old roses are pretty plain and simple compared to the newer ones. And covered with thorns! So Father had all the old roses torn out and just one garden planted with new varieties in the circle of the drive."

"The garden in your paintings? But I didn't see any roses when we drove up."

"They've been gone a long time," Jocelyn

said, and it seemed to Drew that her face had suddenly closed up. She turned to Evan. "Are you as interested in attics and history as Drew is?"

Pandora had come down the back stairway and found them. She was curled in Evan's lap now, purring as he petted her. Evan shook his head.

"Don't blame you. It'll be like digging through a dump, except without the rats. I wish I had lots of suggestions for things you could do around here. I asked about summer programs for kids your age in town—there's a day camp and some events at the library. If you'd like, I could see if we could make arrangements for someone to come pick you up. Shall I?" Evan shook his head. "Not ready for lots of new people?" He shook his head again. "Okay. It's your choice. Let me know if you change your mind." She put the glasses into the dishwasher and closed it. "Just make yourselves at home as best you can. I'd be glad for some help with the chores. There are plenty of books in the library and lots of space outside to explore. The only kid who comes around here is Will. He can take you both on a proper tour of the grounds when he comes on

Monday to weed the daylilies." She turned back to Drew. "Will's pretty near your age. He takes care of the lawn and gardens, such as they are. He'll probably be able to fill you in on whatever you need to know to survive in the teen world of Riverton."

The teen world of Riverton, Drew thought. She expects me to stay. Not like the Tildens.

"You can take Pandora outside exploring with you if you'd like," Jocelyn said to Evan, "as long as she'll stay with you. Just remember, don't get out of sight of the house."

It sounded so ordinary, the way Aunt Jocelyn spoke to Evan, Drew thought. There were no clever tricks embedded in the conversation, no hint of that pitying tone Mrs. Tilden always used.

Home, Drew thought again as they headed out to begin exploring Rose Hill.

CHAPTER
FIVE

SUNDAY HAD BEEN a quiet day, gray and rainy, but not boring, as Aunt Jocelyn had feared. Drew had helped make waffles, learning where things were kept in the kitchen and pantry so she could be useful. Then, while Aunt Jocelyn was with their grandfather, Drew and Evan had done the dishes and cleaned up. Ordinary chores gave her a sense of belonging. Besides, she was determined to keep their presence at Rose Hill from being a burden. Afterward, Evan disappeared into his room and Drew found a book in the library that had been on her summer reading list for two years. She'd spent most of the afternoon in the library, reading in the big comfortable leather chair. The library would be a wonderful place in the winter, she thought, curled in this chair with a cup of cocoa and a good book, with a fire roaring in the fireplace. She imagined Pandora asleep on the hearth, Evan toasting a marshmallow, Aunt Jocelyn sitting in the other chair, knitting, maybe. Or—since she was an artist—sketching.

Now, Monday morning, it was still gray outside, the clouds low and threatening rain again. Will, the boy who'd been going to take her and Evan for a tour of the property, had called to say he'd come in the afternoon if it cleared, or tomorrow if it didn't. So Drew had come to the attic to explore. She sneezed. Aunt Jocelyn had been right about needing a gas mask up here. Dust rose from everything she touched. The first box had turned out to be just what she thought—school papers from Aunt Jocelyn's high school years. Drew hadn't bothered to go further into that box. She wasn't exactly sure what she hoped to find, but it wasn't that.

All year, she'd focused carefully on the present, the current day, hour, minute. In the room she shared with Tillie Tilden, she'd hung a motto where she could see it when she woke in the morning: "Today is the first day of the rest of your life." But in this place, it seemed impossible to shut out the past. She saw it every time she looked at Aunt Jocelyn, thought about it as she climbed the stairs to her room, stairs her father had climbed when he was her age, when he was Evan's age. She could not keep from wondering about why she and Evan had never known about Grandfather, Aunt Jocelyn, Rose Hill. She'd started to ask about it a couple of times, but Aunt Jocelyn had changed the subject before she could finish her question. Whatever had happened, she didn't want to talk about it any more than their father had.

Maybe something up here, she thought as she threaded her way back through the stacks of boxes, would give her a clue.

The old man, her grandfather, seemed so tight and closed off. She could imagine him turning against his oldest son. But why? Could her father, the history and classics scholar, have been a difficult and rebellious teenager? She could hardly imagine the possibility. For that matter, she could hardly imagine him as a teenager.

An image formed in her mind of her father

the way she'd last seen him, sitting at the kitchen table, his hair graying, his face comfortably creased. With that image came another, of her mother standing behind him, coffeepot in one hand, her other resting on his shoulder. Drew pushed the pictures away. She took two long, deep breaths, staring at the pile of boxes in front of her. The concrete reality of now. What she wanted from this place was not her own memory but something further back, something from another time entirely.

She looked into untaped boxes first. Receipts, canceled checks, letters, most of them to Jocelyn. Then she peeled the tape from a sealed box, feeling a little as if she was prying. But Aunt Jocelyn had said she could explore. Opening boxes was exploring, wasn't it? And if there was anything up here she shouldn't see, wouldn't Aunt Jocelyn have told her not to come up?

Nothing inside this box but old magazines— issues of *The New Yorker* from the seventies. She lifted it, surprised at its weight, onto the floor. In the box underneath, she found pages of artwork done by a small child, the paper brittle and crumbling at the edges. She lifted them carefully out. Each was a crayon drawing of an animal, some recognizable (an elephant with a long, lumpy trunk, a vividly striped tiger), some not. Under the drawings she found a yo-yo, some small wooden cars and trucks, and, crushed into the bottom of the box, a big, soft brown-and-white stuffed rabbit. She pulled it out and fluffed it a bit, sneezing again in the dust. The pink satin ears flopped on each side of its head. Though worn in places, it was wonderfully fluffy and soft, and its black bead eyes seemed almost alive above the pink nose and stiff whiskers. The eyes reminded her of her beloved Charley.

She hugged it to her for a moment, feeling its cuddly softness, a comfortable, familiar feeling. How much better this rabbit would be on her bed than Tillie's unicorn. She thought of taking it down with her, except it wasn't hers to take. She could ask Aunt Jocelyn about it, though.

Drew shook the rabbit gently again and began to put it back into the box. But then she stopped. It seemed almost to be asking her not to cage it up again. She stepped over the magazine box and set the rabbit next to the tattered Raggedy Ann on the overstuffed chair. "She'll keep you company for now," she told the rabbit. "You don't have to be crushed into that old box anymore."

She set the box the rabbit had been in on top of the magazine box and pulled the tape off the one beneath. On the corner of the top flap an *A* was printed in black, a circle drawn around the letter. What did the *A* stand for? she wondered. As Drew opened the top two flaps, a heavy, sweet scent rose around her like steam from a pan when the lid is raised. Suddenly, she felt sick to her stomach. She stood for a moment, bent over the box, her hands still on the cardboard flaps, waiting for the nausea to go away.

After a moment, her stomach settled. She opened the lower flaps. Letters, she saw, still in their envelopes, written with a feminine, flowery hand. She reached to take one out and the sweet, sickening smell engulfed her. Nausea swept over her again and the taste of her breakfast cereal filled her throat. She shivered, feeling suddenly not only sick but chilled. Dropping the letter back into the box, Drew stood up straight, one hand on her stomach, swallowing hard. After a moment, the feeling passed. She stood for a bit more, making sure it had gone.

Weird, she thought. She glanced at the rabbit. It seemed almost to be offering sympathy. And she felt perfectly all right again. "Weird," she said to it. "Whatever it was, it's gone."

She picked up the box the rabbit had been in and put it back on top of the other. Whatever the box with the *A* might hold, she had no interest in getting near it again. She'd heard of perfumed stationery, but she was surprised at how strong the perfume could be. Probably it was from being closed up for so long. Maybe she was allergic to it. Or maybe she was coming down with something.

She clicked on the flashlight and shone it over the older, denser stacks of junk, wondering what might still be here from long ago, really long ago. This house had been here before there was electricity, before airplanes or even cars. What might people from that time have left up here?

She considered going back downstairs, finding Evan and seeing what he was doing, or offering to help Aunt Jocelyn. Maybe it was dust, the mustiness, the acrid smell of mouse that, along with the perfumey smell, had made her feel sick. But the nausea was gone. And the old part of the house begged to be explored.

So she pushed her way back into the old house through the stacks of boxes and the discarded chairs and tables. Twice she was stopped by what amounted to a wall of junk, impenetrable and unmovable. An ancient buffet, piled with unshaded lamps, chipped dishes, mildewed books, and jammed against two towering wooden shapes that must have been wardrobes, blocked access to the left side of the old house. Gigantic steamer trunks kept her from reaching the angle of the roof that was directly over the center front door. But her flashlight found a narrow pathway between two tall wooden file cabinets. By turning sideways, she managed to squeeze between, and found herself in a small space under the eaves of the right side of the old house. Stacked against the roof were wooden packing crates approximately a foot in every dimension.

She set the flashlight on one stack and tugged the top box of another stack loose. She set it heavily on the floor. Here, what covered everything was not so much dust as dirt, or soot— black and deep. Drew made a *D* on the lid with one finger and then lifted it.

Inside were stacks of envelopes of different sizes, mostly small, addressed in thin, elegant script. She retrieved the flashlight and put it under her arm as she knelt by the box and took out the top envelope. "Miss Agnes Hildebrand, Rose Hill, New York," it said. A red-and-white stamp with George Washington's picture was pasted on the upper corner; the stamp had cost two cents. Drew tried to make out the blurred postmark but couldn't.

Carefully, she took out the letter folded inside. The paper was heavy and barely yellowed, though the ink that must have been black once was now brown. "Flatbush, July 24, 1888" was written in the upper corner. 1888. This letter was more than a century old.

"Dear Aggie," she read. "Your letter and card gave Willie much pleasure. His birthday was the 9th. Poor boy, he hasn't had any good of his vacation, as he has been sick since the first of the month with scarlet fever. He thinks it was the meanest Fourth of July and birthday he ever had. He will write soon. We think of you often. You owe me a letter. Sincerely yours, Stella."

Drew smiled. This was what her father had said history was—people living their ordinary lives: kids being sick on their birthdays, people owing other people letters. She picked up the next envelope.

This one was addressed with what looked like a calligraphy pen. Inside, there was no letter, only a yellowed newspaper clipping, the print so tiny that she had to hold the flashlight closer to read it. The long, narrow clipping was cut carefully along a double black-lined border.

"Florence E. Sherwin, the eldest child and only daughter of W. F. Sherwin, died at the Rathbun house Thursday afternoon a little after one o'clock, at the age of twenty-one years." Drew stopped reading. Death again. She started to fold the clipping to put it back but then wondered at how long the story was. Had Florence Sherwin been someone especially important to rate nearly six inches of tiny print? She read on. "Less than a year ago, she was a rosy, hearty girl, giving promise of a life of beauty and usefulness. One evening last March, at a church entertainment, she took cold, that rapidly developed into the most dangerous pulmonary complaint, and although all that skill and the most assiduous attention could suggest was done, everything was in vain. The gentle spirit took its flight from the frame too frail to hold it. Consciousness remained almost to the last moment, showing itself, if not in words, in looks and motions." Drew shook her head. She couldn't imagine a modern newspaper printing such personal details. She was glad they didn't. Who wanted to read this sort of thing?

"Services were held this morning. The Rev.

A. B. Riggs made a few remarks and offered prayer. After the singing of a hymn, the remains"—Drew shuddered at the word—"were viewed by many sympathizing friends. Miss Sherwin was dutiful, loving, and lovable in life, and in death her face wore a sweetness of expression which could only be borne by one who had died at peace with all and who realized that a blissful immortality awaited her beyond the grave. There the loved one will be waiting for those who now are stricken with sorrow by their great loss. May not this assurance be some comfort to them as they continue the journey of life?"

Drew closed her eyes. After a moment, she folded the strip of paper, noticing in the flashlight's pale light how dirty her fingers were. Blissful immortality. And what if that wasn't true? What if dead was just dead? Gone. She slipped it back into the envelope, put the envelope in the box, and closed the lid. She brushed away the *D* she'd written on the lid, stood up, and shoved the box roughly back against the slope of the roof with her foot. Some comfort, she thought. *Some comfort.*

CHAPTER

"SORRY, BUT I don't know much about the Hildebrands," Aunt Jocelyn said when Drew asked about Agnes Hildebrand at dinner that evening. "They were the second or third family to live in the house, I think, but they'd left Riverton by the time I was born. Father might know something about them."

Drew shook her head. "Don't bother him about it. It's not important. I just found some letters of hers and wondered what life must have been like here in 1888."

"Letters are a little like time travel, aren't they? People write about all the little details of their lives. I found a diary when I was playing up there once. It was fascinating, I remember, except that it only went as far as March." She looked off as if she was remembering. "I don't remember what I did with it. How far back into the old house did you get?"

"About halfway, I think. It's pretty crowded. I looked at some of the closer boxes first—"

"You probably won't find much that's interesting from our time. I don't think there's anything up there of your father's. Douglas packed up what he wanted after the—" Aunt Jocelyn stopped, as if she'd changed her mind about what she was going to say. Then she cleared her throat. "—When he was here last. He told Father he was welcome to throw everything else away." She reached down to slip a bit of chicken to Pandora, who was sitting between her chair and Evan's. "As far as I know, Father did." She looked up again and saw Evan's expression—eyebrows knitted, mouth severe. "Not supposed to feed the cat at the table, eh?"

"It was a Tilden rule," Drew explained.

Aunt Jocelyn didn't take her eyes from Evan's face. "She's your cat. What do you say? Shall we keep her virtuous and stick with the

Tildens' rule? Or do we spoil her? She's thin enough. I don't think we have to worry about her figure."

Evan glanced down at Pandora, who had finished the bit of chicken and was looking up again hopefully. He wrinkled his nose and nodded.

"Spoil her?" Jocelyn asked.

In answer, he picked a bit of chicken from his own plate and held it out to Pandora. Delicately, her whiskers twitching, the cat took it. Evan and Aunt Jocelyn smiled together. Pandora, apparently satisfied, settled herself on the floor between them, an equal distance from both pairs of legs.

Drew thought of all the dinners at the Tildens', of Evan's pale, expressionless face looking at his plate, avoiding eye contact with anyone as Mrs. Tilden fluttered and chattered and fussed. Dr. Rosenberry should see him now, she thought.

On Tuesday, the clouds had gone and the sun rose into a clear sky. Evan had been late coming down to breakfast, though Drew had called him twice to let him know it was ready. And when she'd asked him if he wanted to go outside exploring with her, he'd shaken his head no. "What are you going to do instead?" she'd asked. "Stay in your room on a gorgeous day like this?" To her surprise, he'd nodded.

"I have to run a couple of errands this afternoon," Aunt Jocelyn told him, "and if Drew will stay here to listen for Father's bell, I'll take you along."

Evan shook his head.

Aunt Jocelyn frowned. "Well, suit yourself. But eventually you'll need to get out a little, or you'll turn into a mushroom. A dull, boring indoor mushroom! Pandora, too."

He grinned, the elfish twinkle in his eyes, and shook his head.

After the kitchen was cleaned up and Aunt Jocelyn had gone to take their grandfather's medicine to him, Evan, with Pandora trailing behind, went back upstairs.

So Drew was on her own again. The two of them had checked out the derelict greenhouse the first afternoon, with its whitewashed windows and the empty places where panes had broken out, and the sheds full of old tools and farming equipment behind the main house. Now she had come through the dim first floor of the carriage house, practically empty except for Aunt

Jocelyn's old station wagon, and found the steep stairs to the second floor.

There were some tires stacked in one corner, and half a wall covered with old license plates. In the front, there was a sliding door where hay must once have been hoisted up to be stored here, when the carriage house had been a carriage house and not a garage. She slid the door open and stood for a moment, looking down. It was a place she would have loved to play in when she was little. Rapunzel's tower, a castle, a fort—the place had almost infinite possibilities.

She gathered a handful of acorns that had lodged in the cracks in the floor and threw them, aiming at a tuft of grass growing up through a crack in the driveway below. As they hit the pavement and scattered, a bicycle skidded into sight, ridden by a lanky boy with a shock of dark hair. He was dressed in faded cutoffs and a T-shirt that said *Riverton Tigers.* He untangled himself from the bike and let it down.

"Don't shoot. I surrender!"

Drew shrugged. "Sorry. I didn't see you."

"The story of my life." The boy grinned, showing a mouthful of braces. "You must be Drew Broderick."

Drew nodded.

"I'm Will Hardin." There was a moment of silence and he put his hands into his pockets. "Your aunt said I should give you a tour. You and your brother."

"Hold on," Drew told him. "I'll come down."

Standing next to the boy, Drew felt short. He seemed to be all arms and legs, with the biggest hands and feet she'd ever seen. "My brother refuses to come out today. You can take me around, and I'll give him his own tour later."

Will nodded, a lock of hair bouncing against his forehead. "Okay. Whatever." He picked up his bike and wheeled it over to lean it against the carriage house.

For the rest of the morning, they wandered the grounds of Rose Hill, sometimes following the dirt road that began at the carriage house and wound down the hill, through woodlands and across meadows, and sometimes following narrower lanes off to the fields that Will's father rented for farming. Will didn't say much as they walked. Drew was busy taking in the sheer beauty of the land, the woods full of low-growing wildflowers and mushrooms—"Toadstools, mostly," Will warned—and the wide, rolling meadows. It was like walking into a nature calendar, except that every sight she saw was a part of Rose Hill.

The farm road ended at another set of iron gates, these closed and padlocked between brick gateposts identical to the ones in the front, even to the Oriental dogs.

"I live down that way." Will pointed down the road to the right. "Dad farms a little land of our own and works your grandfather's fields. He brings his tractor through these gates."

"Why are they locked?"

"Beats me. Your grandfather's rule."

Drew pushed her hair back off her forehead. The sun made walking hotter than she'd expected.

"Tired?" Will asked.

Drew shook her head. "Not really. Just a little hot."

"We could go to the old pond and then back up to the house between Dad's cornfields. There's a shady place by the pond where we could rest awhile before we go back."

"Sounds good."

The lane Will took led off to the left. It was so overgrown with grass and nettles that it was hard to tell it was a road at all. It led through a stand of trees, sloping always downward, and then across a stretch of grass and low shrubs. A thick growth of cattails showed that they must be nearing water. The ground, Drew noticed, began to feel springy. Dampness seeped into the canvas of her tennis shoes. A muddy, rotten smell rose up as she stepped.

"Careful," Will said. "We can't follow the old lane much farther—it gets really mucky. This used to be a regular farm pond, but it's been silting up over the years and isn't much more than swamp now. There's hardly any open water left. Dad says the muck's sort of like quicksand—it could just about suck you in." He angled away from the road and plowed through grass, making a curved way around the cattails. The ground began to slope upward and felt more solid as they headed for a cluster of willow trees on a slight rise. Drew followed and smiled as Will stopped and flung his arm toward the view. "Ta-dah!"

It was mostly swamp, as Will had said, choked with green scum among the cattails, but on this side, against the slope where the trees grew, it was still pond, blue and quiet, reflecting the sky and a high white cloud that was moving slowly overhead. Will offered a seat on a boulder beneath an ancient willow. Drew sat. "There's something creepy about a swamp. Or a marsh, or whatever this is."

Will nodded, leaning against the willow trunk. "The pond's pretty enough, though. A blue heron hangs around, so there must be fish, and I've seen muskrats and turtles. And lots of dragonflies."

After a while, Will slid down and sat against the tree. "Have you always lived here?" Drew asked, feeling awkward as the silence stretched on.

"Just since I was five. We had a little place down near Albany, but the developers were buying everything up and Dad wanted more land, anyway. So we came up here. Where did you—" Will didn't finish the question, and Drew saw that his cheeks had gone pink. "Sorry, I guess maybe you don't want to talk about—it—uh, stuff."

So he knows, Drew thought. She'd hoped maybe somehow he didn't. "It's okay. I grew up in Northridge, Massachusetts. Evan and I came here because our parents were killed in a gas explosion last fall."

"I'm sorry. That's—"

"Awful. Yeah. And you're right, I don't talk about it. This is going to be my home from now on, though, so I want to know everything I can about it. Rose Hill is gorgeous, I think. Don't you? The house, I mean."

Will shoved his hair back off his forehead. He seemed relieved that she'd changed the subject. "Yeah. It's a terrific old house." He paused, looking up at the leaves moving overhead, then added, "Mysterious."

"Mysterious?"

"Oh—you know. Big and old. Dark."

"Beautiful," Drew said.

"Yeah." He picked a grass blade and smoothed it between his fingers. "But there's something eerie about it, too. Downstairs all the windows open and clean and the white curtains at the windows, and upstairs everything closed off."

"Not anymore. Evan and I are upstairs now. That was just because Aunt Jocelyn didn't want to take care of the whole place when she and Grandfather both had rooms on the first floor. Nothing eerie about that."

Will held the grass blade between his thumbs and blew on it to make a high-pitched whistling sound. "There's that weedy place in the middle of the driveway that must have been a garden once. Not eerie, maybe, but sort of weird. I asked if I could plant something there—make the front of the house prettier, you know. Roses, I suggested, for Rose Hill. I mean, there's not a single rosebush on the whole place. I read up on it, because roses are really complicated. But when I told your aunt my idea, she had a fit. You would have thought I'd suggested planting poison ivy or something."

"Maybe she'd just had a bad day. She has a rough time with my grandfather sometimes."

Will nodded. "I've never met him, but Dad says even as sick as he is, he knows how to make his wishes known."

"I guess."

They sat for a while in silence again. Will blew on the grass blade, then dropped it on the ground and picked another. "There's something else weird," he said.

"What?" Drew picked a grass blade of her own and tried to make it whistle.

Will showed her how to hold it. When she blew on it again, it made a brief shrill squeak.

"I was digging out burdocks in the circle one

time, the first week I worked here," Will said, "and I got a feeling someone was watching me." His voice had dropped so low now that Drew had to strain to hear. "I looked around and didn't see anybody, but the feeling didn't go away. Then I glanced up, and there was a woman standing in that center window upstairs, staring down at me. I smiled and sort of nodded, but she just stood there. So I went back to work, and when I looked up, only a second or two later, she was gone. The blind was down and everything was the same as always."

"What's weird? It was probably just Aunt Jocelyn—upstairs to clean or something."

"It wasn't your aunt. This woman had blond hair, very long."

"Somebody visiting, then."

Will shook his head. "I asked your aunt if there was anybody else in the house. She made some joke about how they're so old and boring, they never have any visitors. So I didn't tell her what I'd seen. I was beginning to wonder if I'd really seen anything, anyway. The woman was there and gone so fast."

Drew remembered, suddenly, the feeling she'd had that something had moved on the second floor that first day—something in the center window, just before Pandora howled. Goose bumps rose on her arms.

"I'd just about forgotten about it, when it happened again. The same way exactly. I was working in that circle and there she was, looking down at me. There and then—the moment I looked away—gone. And two more times after that," Will said. "Always in the same window. I see her standing there, and a second later the blind's down. Sometimes—" Will stopped. He picked a handful of grass and let it fall from his hand, scattering on the breeze.

"Well? Sometimes what?"

"Sometimes even when there's nothing there, it's like I feel her...watching."

Drew threw down her grass blade. "So what are you saying? That you think she's a ghost?"

"I don't know."

"Did you tell anybody about her?"

Will shook his head. "I just got some books from the library about ghosts and haunted houses, the ones that are supposed to be real. My father says I've read so much about ghosts now that I'll probably start seeing them flying in and out of our barn."

Drew glanced down at her arms. The goose bumps hadn't quite gone away. "You don't *believe* in ghosts, do you?"

He shrugged. "Lots of people do."

"Let's go back now," Drew said. Suddenly, she wanted to get away from the pond, with its thick fringe of cattails, its scum of green weed.

It didn't take as long to get back, walking on around the pond and up between the cornfields, as Drew had expected. As they walked, they talked about safe things—Riverton High School and music and movies.

When they reached the outbuildings, Drew looked up at the house. She could see the windows of her own room from here, the shade up, the curtains pulled back. Open and inviting. Nothing weird and mysterious about Rose Hill.

"I've got to weed the daylilies," Will said.

"Thanks for the tour."

"You're welcome. See you later." Will angled off toward the greenhouse. At the doorway, he turned back. "I didn't mean to scare you," he said.

"You didn't," Drew answered. She stood for a moment before she went in, looking up at the house. The June sun shone down on the slate roof, making it shimmer with heat waves. It shone on the oak trees, on the garden near the kitchen door. There's nothing at all mysterious about Rose Hill, she thought again. Nothing!

CHAPTER

SEVEN

"BEAUTIFUL, BEAUTIFUL, BEAUTIFUL," Drew said when she went into the kitchen where Aunt Jocelyn was making a lunch tray for her father. "I love it here!"

"Where did you go?"

"Everywhere. Down the road to the back gates, around the pond, up between the cornfields."

Jocelyn's back straightened and her voice was sharp. "You didn't go close to the pond?"

"Just close enough on the old road to get my sneakers muddy, and then we went around to that batch of willows on the little hill. It's pretty from there."

"Just an old farm pond, so small now there's nothing much to look at. Reeds and muck, mostly." Jocelyn turned to look directly at Drew, her eyes intent, her face set in tense lines. "Stay away from the marshy side, you hear? And be sure Evan doesn't go there, either. It's dangerous."

Drew nodded. "That's what Will said. I didn't much like the look of that side, anyway. All that green scum."

"We should have the whole thing filled in. The back gates are kept locked, so nobody's likely to go there, but we probably shouldn't take the chance. Be absolutely sure Evan knows to stay away." She turned back to the lunch tray, setting a small plate of cut-up sandwich pieces on it and placing a folded yellow napkin carefully next to the plate. "Lunch will be ready shortly. You'll want to wash up. And please call Evan down."

"Has he been up in his room all morning?" Drew asked.

Jocelyn sighed and nodded. "I don't think it's a good idea for him to be by himself too much. But I don't like forcing him."

Drew shrugged. Everyone was always so busy worrying about Evan at the Tildens', she hadn't had to think about him much. They always seemed so sure of what he needed. Now, if Jocelyn wasn't sure, Drew couldn't help. "Mrs. Tilden used to force him," she said. "It didn't work."

Jocelyn picked up the tray. "No one can force him to talk, though, can they? Tell him fifteen minutes."

Aware of her muddy sneakers, Drew went up the uncarpeted back stairs. Now, in the middle of the day, it was warm upstairs. She took off her shirt and washed as best she could in the old-fashioned bathroom, wishing it had a shower instead of just a tub, then went to her room to change out of her jeans and sneakers into shorts and sandals. She ran a comb through her hair and then stood for a moment, gazing at the rose garden watercolor. Will had said there were no roses at Rose Hill. The antique roses were gone and the garden in that painting was gone, too. Why? she wondered. It had been so beautiful.

As she turned to leave, she noticed the unicorn leaning stiffly against her pillow and thought again of the big, soft rabbit she had found. Surely Aunt Jocelyn wouldn't mind if she brought it down and put it on her bed. It wasn't doing anybody any good in the attic. She could get it now and ask at lunch. If Aunt Jocelyn didn't want her to have it for some reason, she could always take it back up.

She opened the attic door and started up the steps. The heat even at the bottom of the steps was like a wall. As she climbed toward the landing, it felt more like a hand trying to push her back. Halfway up the second flight, she could feel the perspiration starting. She turned around and went back down. No sense going up for it now, she thought. She'd only just washed off the sweat from the morning.

Drew was surprised to find Evan's door closed. What could he be doing in there? She thought about Aunt Jocelyn's tease. She had a fleeting image of opening his door and finding nothing but a big white mushroom on his bed.

She grinned as she knocked. "Evan?" She heard movement inside, but Evan didn't come to the door. "Evan, Aunt Jocelyn says fifteen minutes till lunch. Ten minutes by now."

She waited for a moment, then opened the door and stuck her head in. Pandora was asleep in the middle of the lion's head quilt. Evan was sitting on the floor, a circle of carved wooden animals around him. She'd never seen them before.

They must have been in the room, she thought. He looked up at her, frowning, and gestured at her to get out. "Okay, okay, but did you hear? Ten minutes till lunch." He nodded and waved her away.

She closed the door. Evan was too big a problem for her to think about. She headed for the red-carpeted front stairs and stopped, looking at the three closed doors across the front of the house. The middle one was the door to the room where Will said he had seen the woman.

He imagined the whole thing, she thought.

A big old house, half closed up, with nobody living in it but a sick old man and the daughter who takes care of him. A kid with a good imagination might think he'd seen a ghost in a window.

But there was no such thing as a ghost. No such thing.

Instead of going down the stairs, Drew found herself walking slowly past the stairwell, her sandals making no sound against the rug. And then she was standing at the door to the room. She listened: nothing. Of course not—how could there be?

She reached out and took hold of the brass

doorknob. *Cold,* she thought briefly as she turned it, *freezing.* The knob turned easily and she heard a click as it unlatched. But the door wouldn't open. She pushed gently. It seemed almost to give a little, as if it was about to open, but then it stopped and would go no farther. She rattled the knob. Nothing. She pushed harder. Though she could see the tiniest space between the edge of the door and the doorjamb, the door simply would not move.

It felt as if something heavy was against the door, keeping it closed. A piece of furniture, maybe. She tried again, leaning against it with her whole body, the knob still icy cold in her hand. For that matter, she realized, her toes in her sandals felt cold, too, as if cold air was pouring out from under the door.

Suddenly, Drew became aware of that same sickly sweet smell she'd noticed in the attic. In moments, she was overwhelmed by nausea again. There was a sour, burning feeling at the back of her throat. She swallowed quickly— once, twice—and leaned her head against the door. What was the matter with her? And where had that smell come from?

The door to Evan's room opened behind her

and she turned, her hand pressed to her stomach. Evan nodded at her and Pandora bounded ahead of him into the hall. Feeling absurdly glad to see them, Drew took a step forward, and as she did, the nausea subsided a little. She swallowed again, and the feeling seemed to go as suddenly as it had come. It was as if just seeing the two of them had made her feel better. Drew grinned. That's probably exactly what it was. She'd gotten herself all worked up with that kid's talk of ghosts and the stuck door and the cold knob. Then Evan and Pandora, so completely real and ordinary, had broken the spell. She crouched and called the cat to her, scratching her finger on the rug to lure her.

Pandora stopped, her green eyes riveted on Drew's moving finger. Slowly, the cat inched forward one step, then another, stalking her prey. She crouched, her front legs and head down, her hindquarters up, watching Drew's movements. Evan stood still, watching, the beginnings of a smile on his face. With a twitch of her rear, Pandora rushed forward to pounce on Drew's hand.

But when she was almost there, the cat stopped abruptly, her body suddenly stiff. A low growl began in her throat and her tail puffed as her back arched. She was no longer looking at Drew's hand, or even at Drew herself, crouched directly in front of her. The cat was looking past Drew at the closed door. The growl began to grow louder. If she yowls like she did before, Drew thought, I'm going to scream!

Evan clucked his tongue at the cat—once, twice, a third time. The growl dwindled and subsided. The cat stood for a moment, her back still arched, and then, still staring at the door, took a single step backward, then another and another. Finally, with a last look at the door, she turned all the way around and went back to Evan.

She rubbed up against his legs and he bent to pick her up, cuddling her against his chest. After a moment, he put her down and raised his eyebrows at Drew. She could almost hear the question he was asking. It was the same as hers: What was that all about?

Drew shrugged. He shrugged, too, and started down the stairs. Pandora, her tail back to normal now, went with him.

Drew stood up. She could almost feel the closed door looming behind her.

It couldn't be a ghost, she told herself. Maybe

there were mice in that room. After all, there were mice in the attic. The cat had probably heard mice scurrying in the room. Drew put her hand on the stairwell railing, glad for the solid, real support of the smooth, polished wood. With the hair prickling up on the back of her neck, she walked slowly and carefully away from the three closed doors. "Lunch," she whispered to herself, to put some human sound into the air. "Time for lunch."

She went to the door Evan had closed behind him when he came out of his room. It had the same sort of brass knob as the door to the center room. Gingerly, she reached out to touch it. Vaguely cool, it felt, with the cool feel of metal. Cooler than the air, certainly. But not cold. Not cold.

CHAPTER
EIGHT

DREW ATE HER lunch almost without tasting it, thinking about that door, thinking about the cold and the strange behavior of the cat. "What's in the center room upstairs?" she asked finally as they were finishing their meal.

"The writing room?" Jocelyn said. "Nothing much. Just a desk and some bookshelves, really. It's not very big. It was a dressing room for the master bedroom, before—" She stopped and got up to clear away the dishes.

Before what? Drew wondered. But Jocelyn didn't finish. "I tried the door, but I couldn't get it open. Is there a piece of furniture up against it?"

Jocelyn shook her head. "Maybe the humidity has swollen the door and it's sticking. Old houses are like that. There's a place in the front hall, under the rug, where the floorboards actually push up and make a sort of miniature mountain range in a really muggy summer."

"Maybe that's it," Drew said. But that wasn't what it had felt like. It had felt like something blocking the door on the inside, holding it closed. *Something or someone.*

She sat for a moment, watching Jocelyn's back as she rinsed dishes and put them into the dishwasher. Evan gathered his plate and glass and took them to the counter. "Do you believe in ghosts?" Drew heard herself asking. She had not intended to mention the word. Evan, his eyes wide, turned to look at her so suddenly that he almost dropped his dishes. She felt silly and a little guilty. She hadn't meant to frighten him.

"You've been talking to Will," Jocelyn said, and laughed. "No, I do not believe in ghosts." She took Evan's dishes from him and patted his shoulder. "I'd have to see one to believe in them—wouldn't you?"

Evan nodded.

"Me too," Drew said, and dropped the subject.

She did not go near the door of the center room again. *Imagination,* she told herself. First Will's and then her own. If she didn't go near, if she didn't think about it, then it was just a door, like the others. Closed, blank, silent. She resolutely pushed all thoughts about the door, about ghosts out of her mind. Instead, she concentrated on settling in at Rose Hill.

Over the next few days, she offered to vacuum and dust, to clean bathrooms, to scrub the kitchen floor. She read. She stayed in the house while Jocelyn ran errands, listening for her grandfather's bell-ringing summons, grateful that the one time she had to answer his call he needed only a drink of water. Grateful, too, that he seemed not to care that she was not Jocelyn, or even to pay particular attention to who she was.

She took Evan on a tour of the grounds, dutifully warning him to stay away from the pond. She took long walks, often going to sit on the stone beneath the willow trees, to watch the heron stalking regally among the reeds or a hawk circling above the pond and the fields. The beauty of Rose Hill's grounds, the calmness and solitude, seemed to warm her whole self, as if she'd been cold inside for a long, long time.

The first time Will came to do yard work, she

found something to do in the house. The second time, Aunt Jocelyn pushed her to go out—"to talk to somebody your own age for a change." Not wanting her aunt to worry about her, as she was worrying about Evan, Drew went. When Will asked if she'd happened to check out the center room, she pretended not even to have thought about his story. "I don't believe in ghosts," she said, dismissing the subject. "Neither does Aunt Jocelyn. And she's lived here all her life. She'd know." They talked about other things then and she helped him weed the gardens. Little by little, Drew began to look forward to the times Will was there. She enjoyed listening to him talk about Riverton High School, his family, the gardening that had begun as a way to make money and then became a real interest.

And she looked forward to the times when their grandfather was sleeping in the late afternoon or evening, when she and Evan and Aunt Jocelyn sat at the kitchen table under the slowly turning ceiling fan and played cards or Clue or Monopoly. Or when Aunt Jocelyn made pencil sketches of them, of Pandora, even of the furniture and dishes. Or the times when they worked together, baking, or cooking, or cleaning up after themselves. Evan developed a kind of sign language, crude but effective. Drew thought Aunt Jocelyn and Evan communicated in other ways, too, sometimes—with their eyes or with touch. Often, Jocelyn reached out and ruffled his hair. When Mrs. Tilden had done that, he would cringe away from her hand. Now it always brought a smile, like a ray of sun piercing clouds.

Then one night, Drew had the nightmare again. It was the same as before—the terror, the need to run, her feet mired in something heavy and sticky. Evan was there, too, and that sense of evil coming after her, after them. She woke in tears, calling for her mother, reaching for Charley. And found only the dark, empty stillness of her room and the stiff form of the unicorn.

She lay there for a long time, clutching the unicorn, reminding herself that she was awake and safe, willing herself to think only about this new life, about everything she loved at Rose Hill. And she remembered the soft brown-and-white rabbit in the attic. She had never asked Aunt Jocelyn about it, never brought it down.

Drew slipped out of bed and went to the door of her room. The attic wouldn't be hot now, in the middle of the night. She could turn on the light, hurry up the stairs, and snatch the rabbit. It would be easier to go back to sleep if she had it with her. She went out into the darkness of the hall, where only the night-light glow from the bathroom held back the shadows, and thought suddenly of that closed center door. She stood for a moment, shifting her weight from one bare foot to the other, peering into the darkness at the front of the house, and then bolted back into her room and closed her door firmly behind her. She got back into bed and pulled the covers up to her chin. "Tomorrow," she whispered to the unicorn that lay rigidly next to her pillow. "I'll ask Aunt Jocelyn first thing tomorrow."

But the next day was one of their grandfather's bad ones. Jocelyn asked Drew to fix breakfast for herself and Evan, and they didn't see her the rest of the morning. Drew tried to get Evan to go out with her to help Will or go for a walk, but he refused. He went, as usual, to his room, with Pandora, as usual, following.

At lunchtime, Aunt Jocelyn came into the kitchen, carrying her father's tray. It looked as if nothing had been disturbed on it. She shook her head. "It's one of those days. He just won't eat.

Not even Jell-O. Not even if I feed it to him. He says he can't swallow it." She set the tray on the counter and sighed again. "Now he probably won't sleep, either. This could be a very long afternoon." She pushed back the tendrils of hair that had come loose around her face and sat down at her own place. The lines around her mouth looked deeper.

"You've never told us what's the matter with Grandfather," Drew said.

Aunt Jocelyn picked up a piece of the ham sandwich Drew had made for her. "He has a form of leukemia. It's quite serious. But it isn't only what's physically wrong with him that causes the trouble—he's depressed and unhappy. Dreadfully unhappy."

"Because he's so sick?" Drew asked.

"Partly. But it goes back a lot further than his diagnosis."

Drew didn't know what to say. "I'm sorry."

Aunt Jocelyn sighed. "So am I. The doctor is doing what he can for the leukemia. But about the rest, the only thing that would help would be to turn back the clock and change his life. The leukemia is new; the unhappiness is very, very old."

Evan reached down and held a carrot stick out to Pandora, who was lying on the floor by his feet. She sniffed it disdainfully and turned away. Jocelyn smiled, and the tiredness in her face seemed to lessen briefly. "She's not a vegetarian, eh? I've heard that some cats like asparagus," she said. "We could make some for dinner and try her on that." She took a bite of her sandwich.

"Did you have a good morning?" Aunt Jocelyn asked Evan when she'd swallowed. Evan smiled and nodded. "In your room again, I suppose." She paused, as if making up her mind whether to say what she was thinking, and then spoke again. "The first Evan used to spend a lot of time there, too. Just him and his books and crayons and stuffed animals." It was the first time she had mentioned her brother since the day they'd arrived.

Stuffed animals, Drew thought. The rabbit from the attic must have been Evan's. "I found a stuffed rabbit in the attic," Drew said. "Was that his?"

"A big brown-and-white one?" Jocelyn asked. She had picked up her glass to drink but stopped now, glass in midair, staring into space beyond Drew's shoulder. "I haven't thought of him for years. What was his name?" She closed her eyes a moment, frowning in concentration. "Bunn! That's it. Bunn, with two *n*'s. Once he began learning to write, Evan was very particular about the spelling. 'Bunn-with-two-*n*'s.' He had lots of animals, but Bunn was his favorite. Where did you find him?"

"In a box—under some artwork and toys. Sort of crushed into it. I put him out next to an old Raggedy Ann doll for company."

Aunt Jocelyn smiled. "Not Raggedy Ann. Lulu. I could never stand having a doll somebody else had named. It always seemed as if when they came with a name, they could never really be mine. So I called her Lulu. She must be a mess—"

Drew jumped as Evan banged down his spoon and got up from his chair. He ran out of the kitchen, into the pantry hall, and pounded up the back steps. Pandora had jumped, too, and was now elaborately licking a paw, as if she had intended all along to sit up suddenly and take a little bath.

"What do you suppose that's all about?" Aunt Jocelyn asked.

Drew shrugged.

A door banged upstairs and they could hear Evan's feet coming down the hall and then pounding back down the stairs. He burst into the kitchen, clutching the rabbit. His eyes were bright, his face pink with pleasure. Drew bit her lip. So Evan had been to the attic, too. And now he had the rabbit. *Her* rabbit. Evan held Bunn out to Aunt Jocelyn and she took it gently.

She smoothed the fur and ran her fingers along the satin-lined floppy ears. "Hello, Bunn." She held it up then and gave it a little shake. "He doesn't seem too dusty, considering."

Drew frowned. Since she'd last seen it, the rabbit had been fluffed. Where it had been crushed and distorted, it was now soft and round. And the dust did seem to have been shaken out of it. It reminded her even more now of Charley. It isn't fair for Evan to have it, she thought. I saw it first.

Their grandfather's hand bell rang. Jocelyn glanced over her shoulder toward his room. The bell rang again, more insistently. She handed the rabbit back to Evan and pushed back her chair. "Excuse me. Bunn can join us for lunch," she said. "I'll be back in a few minutes, I hope."

When she had gone, Evan settled the stuffed

rabbit on his lap and went back to eating his sandwich.

Now that he had it, Drew couldn't very well ask to have it herself. After all, she was fourteen and he was only eight. But she could hardly believe how miserable she felt. She sighed and took a sip of her iced tea. When had Evan gone up to the attic? "The attic's pretty amazing, isn't it?" she said to him. "When did you go up there?"

Evan looked at her, his mouth full of sandwich, and shook his head.

"What?"

He shook his head again and spread his hands in a questioning gesture.

"Are you saying you didn't go up there at all?"

Evan nodded.

"Oh, come on, now. You don't mean to tell me that rabbit came down from the attic all by itself and just turned up in your room."

Evan swallowed and frowned. He looked at the rabbit and then back at Drew. And shrugged.

"Okay, let me get this straight," Drew said. "You haven't been up to the attic at all? Not one single time?"

Solemnly, Evan shook his head.

"And the rabbit was just suddenly there in your room?"

Evan nodded.

"There's nobody else in this house except Grandfather, and he doesn't get out of bed. So if I didn't bring it down, and I didn't—unless I've been walking in my sleep—and Aunt Jocelyn didn't bring it down, and you didn't bring it down, how did Bunn get into your room?"

Evan didn't make any effort to respond.

Pandora stood up, stretched, and came over to rub up against his legs. Evan smiled at Drew, hugged the rabbit with one arm, and picked up the last section of his sandwich.

CHAPTER

NINE

DREW SAT ON an overturned wooden crate in the old greenhouse and turned a broken flowerpot over and over in her hands. The sun made square patches on the floor where it streamed through the broken-out panes in the expanse of whitewashed glass above. Aunt Jocelyn expected to spend the afternoon with her father, Evan had gone back to his room again, and Drew had needed to get out of the house.

Dumb as it seemed, she was furious with Evan for taking the rabbit. And he'd taken it without asking. If she'd done that, it would be sitting on her bed now next to Tillie's unicorn. Besides, Evan had lied—and such a stupid lie, it was clear he didn't even care whether she believed him or not. The rabbit had just appeared in his room all by itself. Of course it had!

She picked at a chip in the flowerpot she held. She didn't know how she could be so upset about that wretched rabbit. Unless it was because she'd been on edge ever since the day Will had talked about ghosts, the day she'd tried to go into that center room. She had tried to forget it, ignore it, but it was always there—every time she went up or down the stairs, every time she passed that closed door. Drew thought about Pandora's reaction that day. There *was* something cold in that room. The cold doorknob. The chill on her toes. The cat, too, must have felt it.

"You planning to try to fix that old pot? Can't be done."

Drew looked up, squinting. Will was a rangy silhouette against the glare.

"Just thinking." She put the pot back on the rickety greenhouse table where she had picked it up from, then stood. "What's on for this afternoon?"

"Weeding again. You have to be on those suckers every day or they'll take over the world. You want to help? On a volunteer basis, of course, as usual."

Drew grinned. "As long as we can talk while we weed. I don't need money. I *do* need somebody to talk to."

"Deal!" He handed her a trowel. "You want gloves?"

Drew shook her head. "I don't think I'm going to work hard enough to need gloves."

"Oh well, I guess you get the help you pay for," Will said, and led the way to the patch of daylilies along the back of the house.

Drew smiled to herself as she followed him. She realized she'd been hoping Will would be working this afternoon. It was time to tell him about the cold, and the cat. She'd been holding it in long enough.

While Will dug around the bunches of daylily leaves, pulling out nettles and thistles that were fighting their way up through the dense green, Drew told him about the cold doorknob, the stuck door, Pandora's strange behavior. As she talked, he shook his head or nodded or clucked his tongue. But never did he give even a hint that he might laugh at her. Finally, she even found herself grumping about Evan snatching the rabbit and then lying about it.

"So?" she said when she'd finished. "What do you think? About the room?"

Will looked at her. "What do *you* think?"

"I don't know."

"Sure you do. You're starting to think there might be a ghost. You already know what I think. Remember, I *saw* that woman in the window. Anyway, the cat clinches it. The cat and the cold. Animals can see ghosts even when people can't. And in just about every single ghost story, there's something about cold." Will stuck his trowel into the ground and turned over a clump of dirt with a flourish. "This is great!"

Drew frowned. "That isn't the word I'd use."

"Okay, listen. Could you take me up to that room? Maybe if I tried, I could get the door open. I could go in with you, see if there's anybody there." Will tossed a nettle aside and sat back on his heels.

Drew shook her head. She didn't think she could face confronting that cold and that room again. "I don't think Aunt Jocelyn would like that."

Will sighed and went back to his work. "You think she knows there's a ghost and doesn't talk about it because she doesn't want to scare you?"

Drew tugged at a dandelion. It wouldn't budge. "No. She doesn't believe in ghosts. And if she did think there was one up there, she wouldn't have put us up there alone with it." The dandelion's root broke and the rest came away in her hand.

Will nodded. "I guess you're right. That doesn't mean there isn't a ghost, though. Not everybody can see them, or sense them. All I know is, I saw somebody up there. And she was beautiful. I wonder who she is—or was. She must have something to do with Rose Hill, or she wouldn't be haunting it. It's supposed to be somebody who died here, in that room, maybe. What did your aunt call it?"

"The writing room. But it hasn't always been that. It used to be a dressing room, she said."

Will brushed the dirt off his gloved hands. "Most of the ghosts I've read about died dramatically—some people think that's part of what keeps them haunting. We could find out who she is, I'll bet. How many people could have died here, even as old as the house is? And if somebody died here, especially if it was a really dramatic story, it would be written down somewhere, wouldn't it? In the newspaper or something?"

Death again, Drew thought. But this was dif-

ferent somehow. Distant and removed, like the
plot of a novel. She felt a twinge of excitement.
The idea of tracking down the identity of a ghost
was a lot more appealing than the idea of going
into a closed-up room to meet one. "I found a
newspaper story from the 1800s in the attic,
about a girl who died of a 'chill.' If someone died
dramatically, I'm sure it would have been all over
the paper. Does Riverton have a newspaper?"

"It only comes out once a week. But I think a
long time ago it used to come out every day. We
could ask at the library. They have them back as
far as they go—the 1700s, I think. Before the
house was built. Maybe the ghost is a woman
who stands in that window looking out because
she's waiting for the lover who jilted her. Maybe
he never came and she hanged herself. In her
dressing room."

"Why does *she* have to be the jilted one?"
Drew asked. "Why couldn't she have been forced
to marry someone she didn't love—maybe the
rich man who built this house for her? And then
she met a handsome, dashing young man and
fell madly in love with him. On the night he was
to come and rescue her, she stood in the window
watching for him, but her rich, evil husband,

who had found out about their plan to run away, burst into her dressing room and shot her through the heart!"

Will stood up. "You read too many romance novels."

"I don't read them at all," Drew retorted, pushing herself to her feet. "I made that up all by myself. So where's the library?"

"Right on the center square in Riverton. We could go Saturday—tomorrow—if you want. My mom has a bike she doesn't use anymore. She'd probably let you borrow it for the summer. There's a Historical Society, too, if we don't find what we want at the library."

"Aunt Jocelyn says the Historical Society would probably love to get their hands on the stuff that's up in the attic. Maybe what we want to know is right up there."

"So invite me up to the attic and we'll look."

"We'd suffocate. It's like an oven up there."

"Invite me someday when it's raining, then. It'll be cooler when the sun isn't pounding on the roof. You could tell your aunt that I've come to help you clean up there or something. I'd be better at that than you are at helping me weed, that's for sure."

Drew looked at the tiny pile of weeds she'd pulled out and the heap Will had managed. The ground was freshly turned over around all the lilies, and she had barely gotten any dirt under her nails. "Sorry."

Will grinned. "No problem. I'm the one getting paid."

CHAPTER
TEN

AFTER DINNER, JOCELYN went to try reading her father to sleep. Evan closed himself and Pandora into his room. Drew decided that since it was still light outside and much cooler, she would see if she could find anything in the attic that might provide a clue to the identity of the ghost. *Possible ghost,* she reminded herself firmly. Her flashlight on to supplement the light of the bulb overhead and the sunlight filtering into the old house, she felt the heat growing as she climbed the stairs. But it was not as suffocating as the day she had turned back because of it.

What might turn her back now, she thought

when she got to the top, was the sight of the shadows looming around her. She could feel her heart beating and her breath speeding up as she began to wind her way toward the stacks of wooden boxes under the eaves. She was glad, at least, that her progress was taking her into the lightest part of the attic. "Keep me company," she said out loud, picking up Lulu as she passed the overstuffed chair. The painted smile and button eyes of the old doll gave her a surprising sense of comfort. Lulu was real, she thought. Cheerful and solid and dirty and real.

When she reached the boxes, she pulled out the one she'd gone through before and sat on it, settling Lulu on the floor beside her. She pulled out another and started sorting through letters, bills, receipts, even advertising circulars. Nothing dramatic there. She stacked the letters next to Lulu and opened another box.

Here, she found school papers, composition books full of laboriously copied poems and "moral sayings," letters and more letters. People seemed to have spent so much time writing about their lives, she began to wonder how they found time to live them. She scanned a few of them. But there were no references to runaway

wives or daughters, to murders or mysterious
deaths. Instead, she found notes about how well
(or poorly) vegetable gardens were doing, com-
plaints about the weather, talk of the difficulty of
traveling and the squabbles, sicknesses, and
school triumphs of a great many children.

What she found far too many of were small
black-bordered envelopes holding black-bordered
cards announcing deaths. Some were old people,
uncles and aunts, grandparents, elders of the
church. Others were children who had been
taken off through illness—diphtheria, scarlet
fever, even measles. One card, larger than most,
listed an entire family, parents and six children,
who had died in a house fire in Riverton.

At that one, Drew very nearly abandoned her
search. Visions came flooding back—the police-
man waiting in the principal's office when she'd
been called out of class; the charred ruins of their
house, yellow plastic ribbon draped from sawhorse to sawhorse, making an impenetrable border around the bits and pieces of her shattered
life; the lines of sad faces looming at her one after
the other at the memorial service.

She looked down at the card she held in her
hand, reading the names of the children: Hazel,

Ernestine, Thomas, Isaac, Charles, and Elizabeth-Ann. A voice seemed to speak aloud in her mind: "How fortunate the explosion didn't come an hour earlier, when the children were still at home." Mrs. Eberson from the church had said that and Drew had suddenly found herself outside the chapel, her face pressed into the rough bark of a flaming maple tree. She had not gone back. Mrs. Tilden had come and taken her home, where Evan had been sitting in a huddled ball next to Tillie on the couch, staring blankly at a TV sitcom.

She put the card back in its envelope, then into the box.

The attic cooled and darkened until the little pool of light cast by her flashlight seemed to make the shadows even darker. Drew looked up from a letter describing a church service during which a famous abolitionist had given a speech; she noticed the darkness. What if there really was a ghost? And what if it didn't just stay in the writing room? What if it liked to go where old things were? Like a dark attic?

Hurriedly, her hands shaking, she gathered the stacks of letters she hadn't yet looked at. "I can read these in my room," she told Lulu. "With all the lights on and the door closed!" She put the top on the final box, shoved it back in place, and picked up Lulu. Leaving the other boxes scattered, she made her way back to the attic steps, her breath coming in short gasps as she tried not to think of a ghost gliding upward toward her. She shone the flashlight down the steps—nothing. No ghostly shape materializing, no cold. Gratefully, she clattered down the steps and burst out into the hall.

Evan's door was closed, but the crack of light at the bottom showed that he was still up. "You okay in there?" she called to him. She took the answering thump for a yes. Of course he was okay. She deposited the letters on the desk in her room, settled Lulu next to the unicorn on her bed, and went down the hall to the bathroom.

She washed the soot and dirt from her hands and her face, where she'd brushed her hair back and left black streaks. On her way back to her room, she stopped outside Evan's door. Had she heard something? A voice? She stood for a moment. Silence.

Of course not, she thought. Unless Aunt Jocelyn had come up, who could be talking in Evan's room? Certainly not Evan! She went on to her own room, where she turned on the over-head light and every single lamp, spread out the letters, and began to read.

An hour later, she looked at her clock, startled to see how long she'd been sitting there absorbed in the lives of people who had probably died before even her grandfather had been born. She had found one possibility, though it wasn't the kind of dramatic story Will said ought to be associated with a haunting.

The son of the man who had built the house had gone off on a whaling ship and had not returned. She had found a letter to the boy's father from the owner of the ship line, explaining that though the ship had indeed returned to port at the expected time, his son had not been aboard. There was another, dated six months later, from the captain, explaining that several crewmen had left the ship in the tropics, acquired a fever, and been unable to make the return voyage. The captain did not have any news, but it was assumed that they had died of the fever, as they had not been reported joining any other crew. The letter ended by extending condolences to "Jonathon's grieving parents."

From the dates on the letters, Drew could tell

that it had taken nearly a year for the parents to get this news, and she imagined a mother waiting and wondering all that time, only to learn that her son had probably died on some island halfway around the world. Could the mother be the woman at the window? Waiting through all the years since to see whether her son would come home? It seemed the only possibility in everything Drew had read. She'd tell the story to Will and see what he thought.

That story would be in the local newspaper, she decided. The residents of Rose Hill would always have been prominent figures in Riverton, so the fate of one of the sons of the family would surely be considered worthy of mention.

Still thinking of the parents trying to find their son, Drew slipped into her pajamas and went out into the hall to go to the bathroom. And thought she heard a voice again, coming from Evan's room. She stood for a moment, her hand on her own doorknob, listening. Yes, there it was again, faint but audible. Singing.

Had Aunt Jocelyn come to say good night? Was she singing Evan to sleep?

She crept to his door and stood there holding her breath, her ear close to the wood. It was singing, all right, but not Aunt Jocelyn. The voice was too light to be Aunt Jocelyn's. Was it Evan? It had been so long since she'd heard his voice, she wasn't even sure what it sounded like anymore. She didn't recognize the song.

Drew imagined Mrs. Tilden hearing this. She'd surely burst in on him and hug him till his bones rattled, tears streaming down her cheeks. It's what she'd been working for all these months, with her tricks and traps. Drew smiled. After so short a time at Rose Hill, here was Evan singing.

Maybe because being mute doesn't get him any special attention here, she thought. Because Aunt Jocelyn treats it as perfectly normal. She tiptoed on down toward the bathroom. No sense in letting him know she knew. If he was singing to himself, he'd probably be talking soon enough.

On the way back from the bathroom, Drew listened again. The voice was still there, still singing—a different song now. "Grief's an individual thing," Aunt Jocelyn had said. Did this mean Evan was getting over his? As she had gotten over hers? The images began pushing at the edges of her mind again. Drew pushed them back. Instead, she focused her mind on the story she'd found in the old letters.

She looked toward the dark front part of the house, at the three closed doors. *Your son isn't coming back,* she thought toward the center door. *You don't have to keep waiting for him.*

CHAPTER
ELEVEN

"WAITING FOR HER son to come back from a whaling voyage?" Will asked as he and Drew put their bikes into the bike rack in front of the Riverton library. "That isn't a very dramatic reason for haunting a house for over a hundred years."

"Maybe she was a very devoted mother," Drew said, stretching her sore legs. At Aunt Jocelyn's insistence, she had spent the morning walking all over Rose Hill with Evan, to get him out of the house and into the fresh air. Then it had turned out to be farther to town than she'd thought. And hillier. Luckily, Will's mother's bike was a twelve-speed. "Anyway, her son never did come home. So it *is* dramatic. He died on some tropical island somewhere and she couldn't even go visit his grave. So maybe she hasn't been able to accept his death all these years."

Will threaded a cable through both bikes' tires and clicked a padlock into place. He stood up then, with a puzzled frown. "But if she's a ghost, she's dead. And if she's dead, she knows her son is, too, right? Isn't that the point? Didn't she— how do people say it—'join him in death'? So why would she still stand at the window? Unless the whole thing is a kind of replay of something that happened in the house a long time ago. Some people think houses can soak up really strong emotion and then play it back again—like a kind of videotape—for years and years and years."

Drew shrugged. "So then there isn't a ghost at all?"

"I didn't say I believed that replay thing. I think it's a ghost. A beautiful one. Let's go see if we can find out who she is."

They headed up the steps and into the old stone library building. Will led the way to the reference desk, where a heavyset woman in a flowered dress smiled at him. "What are you after now, Will? More gardening books?"

"Nope. I know everything there is to know about gardening now, thanks to you. We're looking for history. Mrs. Connelly, this is Drew Broderick. She's come to live at Rose Hill."

The smile on the woman's round, cheery face grew broader. She stood up and came out from behind her desk to shake Drew's hand, a pair of half glasses on a gold chain bouncing on her ample bosom as she came. "Joan Connelly," she said. "I'm an old friend of your aunt's. A classmate at least. Kindergarten right through high school graduation, as it turned out." She paused to take a breath, put her glasses on, and looked Drew up and down. "So you're Douglas's daughter. I can see the Broderick, all right. I heard you and—your brother, is it?" Drew nodded. "I heard you were coming, and I'm so glad to meet you. It's good to have Douglas's children back home." Her face changed suddenly, as if she'd remembered the reason Drew and Evan had come, and her blue eyes clouded over. She held on to Drew's hand. "I'm terribly sorry about your parents. Such a terrible accident. Such a tragedy!"

Drew nodded again. She never knew what to say to such a statement.

The woman sighed and patted Drew's hand.

"Some people around here call it the Broderick curse, but you mustn't listen to them. There's no pattern to tragedies like that. Sometimes they just seem to pile up. Even with the Kennedy family, I just don't believe there's such a thing as a curse. People are trying to explain the unexplainable, that's all. Think about it; nothing's happened to a Kennedy for years. So you just put it out of your mind."

How could she put it out of her mind, Drew wondered, when she didn't have any idea what the woman was talking about?

"We're looking for some history about Rose Hill," Will said.

"What sort of history?" the woman asked, finally letting go of Drew's hand. "The house? The grounds? The people who've lived there?" Her attention seemed to wander away from Drew and Will, as if she was already planning her search, mentally pulling books off the shelf.

"Old history. We don't know exactly what we're looking for," Will said. He wasn't going to tell her about the ghost, Drew hoped. Here in this bright library full of books and information, the idea of a ghost seemed totally ignorant and crazy. "Anything dramatic that might have happened there a long time ago. Interesting, memorable."

"It's for a paper I need to make up for my old school," Drew said, and caught Will's wink.

Mrs. Connelly frowned, her eyes nearly disappearing behind her cheeks. "Interesting, memorable. Well, whatever you're after, it'll be in the *Riverton Times*. We have it on microfilm. I hope you aren't in a hurry. Rose Hill was built in the early 1800s, wasn't it? It'll take forever to go through all those papers. How close do you want to come to the present?"

"Not very," Will said. "It has to be something historical."

Mrs. Connelly shook her head. "We'll see what we can find."

"Did you ever hear about a boy who went away on a whaling ship and then didn't come back?" Drew asked.

"Jonathon Vanderbrink! Now why didn't I think of that? It's a famous story in Riverton. There's a plaque over in Town park about him. He went off on a whaling ship—against his father's wishes, I think. He died in the South Seas and his parents didn't know about it for the longest time. More than a year, I think." Mrs. Connelly took her glasses off and rubbed the bridge of her nose. "Imagine what it must have been like back then. If somebody went off on a ship, you didn't hear from them again for months, even years. We're so spoiled with our telephones and beepers and faxes." She shook her head. "When they finally got the news, the Vanderbrinks had a memorial service for him that the whole town turned out for, and the plaque was put up in his memory. That was in the 1850s. We'll see what we can find. That might be just the kind of story you're after."

Drew followed Will and Mrs. Connelly into a small room with two microfilm readers, but she wasn't thinking about the boy on the whaling ship, or even the ghost. She was thinking about what Mrs. Connelly had said about a Broderick curse. What did that mean? Her grandmother had died of polio and a little boy named Evan who would have been her uncle had died in an accident. And then, of course, her parents. Was there more? With an effort, she focused her attention on the explanation Mrs. Connelly was giving about putting the microfilm on the readers.

It took less than an hour to find the newspaper stories about the disappearance of Jonathon

Vanderbrink. Will and Drew put two chairs together so they could both see the screen and read all the newspaper told of the story.

"I don't think that could be it even if a ghost is just a replay," Will said when he'd finished. "She had seven other children. A woman with that many kids couldn't very well just hang out in the window watching for the oldest one to come back."

"Probably not."

"Guess we'll have to come up with some other way to find out about that ghost. You look like you could use an ice-cream cone or something," Will said. "Let's get a cone and then we'll take the scenic route back. I'll show you the sights, such as they are."

Drew groaned. "If the scenic route is longer and hillier than the way we came, forget it. I'm not sure I can make it back as it is. We have to check out the children's section before we go. Evan's been spending most of his time in his room, and Aunt Jocelyn wants him at least to have some new books. She asked me to try to find something funny."

They gave the microfilm back to Mrs. Connelly, assuring her they'd found exactly what they needed. Will thanked her profusely and promised to come back if it turned out they needed more. "You have to be careful with her," Will whispered as they went past the main desk, toward the children's wing. "If you even hint that you haven't found what you want, she'll bury you. You should have seen all the stuff she brought me when I asked her an innocent question about planting roses."

Ahead of them, Drew saw a bright yellow room full of bookshelves and beanbag chairs, with soft-sculpture characters from children's books hanging from the ceiling. It looked warm and welcoming and fun. She was just thinking that she should bring Evan with her next time, wondering if he could ride on the luggage rack of Mrs. Hardin's bike, when she noticed the words carved into the wooden archway between the main room and the children's section: THE AMALIE AND EVAN BRODERICK WING. She touched Will's arm. When he stopped, she pointed.

"Oh, wow," he said. "I'd forgotten about that."

"Amalie and Evan Broderick," Drew said. "Who's Amalie?"

"You got me."

CHAPTER
TWELVE

"I GOT EVAN'S books from the Amalie and Evan Broderick Wing," Drew said at dinner that night. "Is that *our* Evan Broderick? Your little brother?" She caught Aunt Jocelyn's slight nod. "So who is Amalie? You never mentioned her. Did you have a sister, too?"

Jocelyn's face did not change, but it looked as if she kept it that way with an effort. When she answered, her voice was tight. "Amalie was Father's second wife, our stepmother."

"I didn't know you had a stepmother."

In the long silence before Jocelyn spoke again, Drew noticed that Pandora, curled on a chair cushion in the corner, was purring gently. "She wasn't with us long. I find it difficult to talk about that time. The past is the past, and I've done my best to put it behind me." She paused again, and for a moment Drew was afraid she would say no more. With a sigh, Jocelyn went on. "Amalie and Evan died together. In the same accident."

"What kind of...accident?" Drew asked. She glanced at Evan and saw that he was looking down at his plate, moving lima beans with his fork. *Accident* was one of those words the Tildens avoided using around him.

Jocelyn wiped her mouth with her napkin and put it next to her plate. "It's the reason I've warned you both so seriously about the pond. Amalie and Evan drowned in that pond. As I've told you, it's very dangerous."

She pushed back her chair. "Excuse me. I think I heard Father's bell." With that, she stood and hurried out of the kitchen, down the hall toward their grandfather's closed door.

Evan pointed to his ear and looked questioningly at Drew. She shook her head. "I didn't hear anything, either."

The ringing of the telephone on the wall next

to the refrigerator startled both of them. Drew realized the phone had not rung a single time since they'd been here. At the Tildens', Drew would have hurried to answer it in case it was one of her friends, to keep Tillie from chattering at them for half an hour before handing over the phone. Here, she knew it couldn't be for her. She waited for Aunt Jocelyn to answer in their grandfather's room.

It was a surprise when Jocelyn called, "Drew, it's Will. Pick it up in there."

"So, what did you find out?" Will asked when she'd said hello. "Who's Amalie?"

"Will, for heaven's sake, we're just eating dinner."

"Sorry. You want me to call back later?"

Drew grinned. She *did* have someone to call her here, someone who'd call back if she couldn't talk right now. "No, that's okay. There isn't much to tell you, so my food won't get cold. Amalie was Jocelyn's stepmother. I guess that makes her my stepgrandmother, if there is such a word."

"So? Where is she?"

"Nowhere. I mean, she died in the same accident the first Evan died in. They drowned in the old pond."

There was a brief silence on the other end. "I'm sorry. I guess that would explain why your aunt's paranoid about it. My dad offered to dredge it out for them, turn it back into a real pond. He says she just about took his head off. You better get back to your dinner. I didn't mean to interrupt."

"That's okay." Suddenly, Drew had an idea. "Will, would you ride to the library with me again on Monday? I want to talk to Mrs. Connelly some more." Mrs. Connelly had known Aunt Jocelyn all her life. And given how she talked, she'd almost certainly tell whatever she knew about Amalie and Evan. Whatever it was that Aunt Jocelyn wanted to forget, it probably had something to do with the Broderick curse. And Drew wanted to know more.

Drew heard Will sigh, but he didn't answer at first. She waited. "I was planning to work Monday—"

"That's okay. I'll help. We can go as soon as we get done."

"But Mrs. Connelly'll talk your arm and both legs off if you aren't careful. She's bad enough on subjects she has to look up. What'll she be like about something she actually remembers?"

"That's the whole point. Who better to tell me what Aunt Jocelyn won't?"

"Oh, all right. But we work first."

Monday morning, Aunt Jocelyn sent Evan out along with Drew to help Will. Drew had explained to Will about Evan not talking, so he did his best not to make a big deal about it. But when he started talking slowly and especially loud, she had to remind him that Evan could hear all right, he just didn't talk. Will blushed furiously, but after that, everything was easier.

They dug compost into the earth around the peonies and the irises and then weeded the herb bed. While they worked, Pandora lazed in the sun and watched them, making chirring noises at the birds who came to the feeder that hung from the lowest limb of the oak tree next to the kitchen. Drew watched Evan pull on Will's shirt and point to ask whether a shoot was a weed or an herb, and she wondered, since he had begun to sing to himself in his room, why he still wouldn't talk.

Aunt Jocelyn invited Will to join them for lunch. Grandfather had had a good morning and she'd had some time to herself. She showed them a pencil sketch she had made of finches at the bird feeder.

"That's great," Will said.

Drew couldn't help wishing for color. "You could paint them, couldn't you? In watercolors?"

Jocelyn shook her head. "I don't do watercolors anymore. Painting makes too much mess. I can sketch anywhere, anytime."

She meant she could sketch in her father's room, Drew realized. And she wondered how long the old man had been sick, how long Jocelyn's life had had to revolve entirely around him.

After lunch, Drew and Will pedaled into town. "I'm going to keep looking for an explanation of your ghost," Will said as they went in through the huge front doors. "You're on your own with Mrs. Connelly. You can tell me everything she tells you later in about one-tenth as many words."

He headed for the microfilm room as soon as they were inside, with a quick wave in Mrs. Connelly's direction, and Drew went alone to the reference desk.

"It's a long, sad story," Mrs. Connelly said when Drew, settled in a chair across her desk, asked about Amalie and Evan.

"That's okay," Drew said. "If you've got time to tell it, I've got time to listen. Our father never told us about his family. And Aunt Jocelyn won't talk about it at all."

Mrs. Connelly frowned, her blue eyes sad. "She never would. I guess she doesn't want to have to relive it. She's spent her whole life since then trying to make amends. To pay him back."

"Pay who back? For what?"

Mrs. Connelly glanced up at the clock, looked around to see if anyone else needed her, and then settled herself more comfortably into her chair. When she spoke, her voice was low, and Drew had to lean forward to hear.

"Everybody thought Amalie Broderick was just about the best thing that ever happened to Riverton, and to your grandfather. He'd been grieving over his wife's death and hiding out in his work—completely ignoring his children, including poor little Evan—when he met Amalie out west somewhere on a business trip. I guess it was love at first sight, because he brought her back here a little while later and they got married.

"She took to this town like you wouldn't believe. Joined just about every social group and started using Broderick money to help anybody who needed anything. She organized fund-raisers for the hospital and arranged for a whole program of arts events to be presented in the high school auditorium.

"She was a poet herself and loved the arts. Pretty soon, half the people in Riverton were claiming to love the arts, too, and everybody who was anybody was not only attending all the events she'd organized but helping to sponsor them, raising money. People gave money to the library and Amalie persuaded the board to buy volumes of poetry and subscribe to all the poetry journals. Those old geezers just keeled over and did anything she asked. I mean, Amalie Broderick hit this town like a whirlwind."

Mrs. Connelly leaned forward in her chair. "She was just amazingly beautiful, which accounts for a lot. When it first got around that your grandfather had met some young thing and was planning to bring her back here, people talked. You know how they do—a beautiful young woman and a rich middle-aged widower. But then they met her. It was as if the whole town fell in love with Amalie on sight.

"But it wasn't only that she was beautiful.

She was different—dramatic. The fifties weren't a very exciting time in fashion. Women were wearing something called the 'sack dress,' and that's about what they looked like—sacks. Amalie just ignored the fashion. I think she probably had her dresses made for her somewhere—out west, maybe, wherever it was she came from. They were all soft and flowing and flowery. Light and shimmery. When she walked, she sort of floated along."

Mrs. Connelly gave a slightly embarrassed chuckle. "Maybe that's just the teenage me remembering. I was in junior high when she came, and I'd have been willing to die to look like Amalie Broderick. The way I'd wanted to look like Audrey Hepburn before Amalie came to town." She glanced down at her broad self, gave a little laugh, and shook her head.

"Anyway, Amalie moved into Rose Hill and took on the raising of those three children—well, no, not all three. Your father was too old for that. He was already off in college. He just came home for the wedding. As I remember it, he was the only one who wasn't crazy about Amalie. People said he couldn't stand the thought of *anyone* taking his mother's place, not even Amalie.

"Jocelyn was in my class, like I said, so she

was just fourteen when they married. Evan must have been five, and he'd been pretty traumatized by the loss of his mother—" Mrs. Connelly broke off. "I'm sorry. After what you and your brother have been through, maybe you'd rather not hear about all this."

"That's all right," Drew said. "It's my family. I want to know."

"If you're sure. It's a painful story."

"I'm sure."

"Well, Evan had lost his mother, and then the way his father dealt with his own grief, shutting out everything except work—that made everything harder. Gilbert hired a full-time housekeeper, but Evan had been pretty much alone, with Jocelyn acting as a baby-sitter a good part of the time—as if she didn't have enough grief herself, poor thing. I mean, her mother had died, too."

Drew's stomach twitched. Yes.

"But Amalie swept into their lives and took over Rose Hill the way she took over Riverton, giving her all to the two children who were still there. Jocelyn was a real artist—did you know that?"

Drew nodded.

Mrs. Connelly gave a little satisfied sniff.

"Real talent, it was. And Amalie saw that right away. She knew that kind of talent couldn't get very far in Riverton. There wasn't a teacher in the high school who knew how to take Jocelyn where that talent could get her. So they decided to send her to a boarding school somewhere with a specialty in the arts."

Someone came over to ask a question and Mrs. Connelly paused a moment to answer it. Then she looked back at Drew. "Where was I? Oh, yes, the art school. Well, in some ways that may be what caused the whole thing." She paused and stared off into space for a moment. "Jocelyn had a boyfriend she hated having to leave, even though she wanted to go on with her art. One night at the very end of the summer before she was supposed to go—that would have been just before our freshman year—she was baby-sitting for Evan, and her boyfriend, Johnny Deloro it was—now there's a name I haven't thought about in a long time—he came over while she was watching Evan. Your grandfather was off on a business trip and Amalie had gone to visit a sick friend. That's the kind of person she was—always doing something for somebody.

"I guess Jocelyn and Johnny were paying a

lot more attention to each other, since they were about to be separated for a whole school year, than they were to Evan. And for some reason, Evan went off to the pond." Mrs. Connelly thought for a moment. "I remember! Amalie had found a family of foxes. They had a den back by the old pond. She showed Jocelyn where it was so she could go out there and sketch them. Evan had a real thing about wild animals, you know? So Amalie had taken him out to watch them a couple of times. Anyway, the moon was full that night, and Evan probably got it into his head that night would be a good time to see the foxes. So he went out by himself. And somehow he got into the marshy place.

"Nobody knows for sure what happened, but they pieced it together later. They found Amalie's car on the road not far from the back gate into the property. You know where that is?"

Drew nodded.

"Her car had a flat tire. She was probably coming back to get help with the car when she heard Evan floundering around in the marsh. Must have seemed like a providence to her, her happening to be walking back just when he was in trouble out there. Apparently, she went to help him out and got stuck herself. Anyway, they both drowned. Nobody even knew they were gone till Jocelyn went to tell Evan it was time for bed and he wasn't there. They found Amalie's car that night after Jocelyn and Johnny had tried to find Evan and couldn't and then tried to call Amalie where she was supposed to be. Jocelyn called the police when she heard that Amalie hadn't made it to her friend's house. They found the car, like I said, but they didn't find the bodies till the next day." Mrs. Connelly stopped, her eyes misty.

Finally, she sighed a huge sigh. "Gilbert Broderick never got over the loss of Amalie and Evan. He built that wing on the library and dedicated it to their memory, but not long after that he retired and he's never done much of anything since. Jocelyn and Johnny broke up, and Johnny left Riverton the day after graduation. Got a job in Chicago, I heard. Jocelyn didn't go to that art school. She said she didn't want to anymore. Never even went to college. She just stayed home to take care of her father—like she was trying to make it up to him.

"Your father came back for the funeral, and something must have happened between him and Gilbert, because he never came back again. Not once." She stopped and wiped her face with a handkerchief she'd retrieved from her sleeve. "That's the story."

"And that's what started people talking about a curse?"

Mrs. Connelly nodded. "People get ideas. It all seemed just too sad and too fated. The coincidence that Amalie happened to be where she might have rescued Evan, and then, instead, drowning with him. Just so awful, people thought it had to be an evil fate. Then when we heard what happened to your parents—well..."

"So awful, it had to be an evil fate," Drew said. Yes.

"Oh, my dear, I'm sorry. It's such a tragedy—"

"It's all right. Thank you for telling me. I can see why Aunt Jocelyn doesn't want to talk about it." It was worse than just losing somebody you cared about, Drew thought, thinking that what had happened was your fault.

"All that talent gone to waste," Mrs. Connelly said. "And it isn't as if the old man has been grateful all these years." Then she brightened a bit. "Stop in the poetry section of the Amalie and

Evan wing before you go. Your grandfather had a volume of Amalie's poetry printed after she died—a limited print run. The original journal, with the poems in Amalie's own handwriting, is in a glass case in the poetry section. You can check out one of the bound copies if you want. Not much circulation on them, truth be told. Or the whole poetry section, for that matter. Riverton's not a very poetic town, really."

"Thanks." Drew felt drained, more as if she'd gone through the story than if she'd only heard it. She shook hands with Mrs. Connelly and went to find Will.

"So? What did you find out?"

She told him a highly condensed version and he whistled. "Sad!"

Drew nodded. "Let's go find her poetry."

They went back into the brightly colored children's room and the librarian pointed to the far end of the room, where a section of three stacks was separated from the rest by a low railing. A sign on the railing announced it was the poetry section. At the other end, against the wall, there was a wood-and-glass case, lighted from above. Inside was an open journal, its lined pages covered with a looping script. Above the journal was a photo of Amalie Broderick. Drew had just begun to read the poem the journal was open to when Will, behind her, gasped.

"Drew! That's her! That's the ghost!"

CHAPTER

THIRTEEN

"ARE YOU SURE?" Drew looked at the photograph, at the slim oval face with the elegant patrician nose and the pale, pale wavy blond hair slanting over one eye and hanging well past the shoulders. The photo showed Amalie from the waist up, leaning languidly, artistically, against the trunk of a huge tree.

"Of course I'm sure. You don't forget a face like that—hair like that. And that's the kind of thing she was wearing, too."

Drew stared at the photo. "She's beautiful all right." It was the sort of beauty, she thought, that you expected to see in an old painting or on the cover of some elegant fashion magazine, not on a live person you might actually know. "But why would she be haunting Rose Hill?"

Will shrugged. "We could ask her."

"Will!"

"Why not? I mean, I don't know if ghosts can actually answer, but she must be hanging around for a reason. We could at least try."

Drew shuddered and shook her head. The idea of a ghost was one thing. But looking at a real photo of a real woman and believing that woman was now a ghost, an actual ghost that Will had seen and recognized, was something else.

"Listen, ghosts haunt for a reason. Maybe it's only that they haven't realized they're dead. That could be true of Amalie, maybe, because she was so young. Or they stay because they died with some business unfinished and they want to finish it before they go. And sometimes they stay to tell somebody something important. If she had a reason to stay all this time—when did you say she died?"

"August 1961."

"More than thirty years. If she has a reason, we ought to give her a chance to tell us what it is.

It's not a good thing, to be a ghost. I've read that a haunting always means that somebody got stuck between their life on earth and where they're supposed to go next—wherever that is. The afterlife. Heaven probably in this case, from what Mrs. Connelly said. Do you believe in heaven?"

Drew felt her fingers tighten on the edge of the display case. She didn't like thinking about it. When people died, they were gone. Gone so completely and so finally that they might never have been there in the first place. So what did it matter if there was another life after? In heaven or anywhere else? Everything that had ever mattered to them and everyone they ever mattered to got left behind. "I don't know," she said, her voice stretched tight. She concentrated on reading the first verse of the poem the book was open to.

> *Palest golden rose,*
> *You face the setting sun*
> *As if to worship one*
> *Whose dying light flows*
> *Life and color down*
> *On weary souls below.*

Drew didn't know much about poetry, but she didn't think if she found these lines with no idea who wrote them that she would bother to read on.

"Let's find one of the printed copies of her book," she said, and turned toward the shelves, glad for an excuse to move away from Will and the feel of his question still hanging in the air.

There were four copies on the shelf, thin volumes bound in heavy library bindings, the title in gold on the blue spines: *Blooms of Life.* They did not look as if they'd been read much. She pulled one down and opened the stiff covers. There was a cracking sound from the spine. The same photo faced the title page. Will took another copy down and began scanning it.

"Mmmph," he said after a moment. "I see why it was privately printed. I'll bet these couldn't have gotten published any other way."

"My English teacher last year told us fashions change," Drew said, "in poetry like anything else."

"Not that much," Will said.

Drew grinned and nodded. She was glad somehow that neither of them liked the poems. It made Amalie Broderick more human. However beautiful, charming, generous, and loving she might have been, at least she hadn't been a poetic genius, too!

On the way home, the slim volume tucked into her backpack, Drew was almost surprised to hear herself agreeing, as they rode slowly along, to let Will try to talk to the ghost. He had pointed out that Amalie had been such a kind and loving person when she was alive, she was sure to be a kind and loving ghost.

"Okay. We could use that idea you had before, I guess—tell Aunt Jocelyn you're going to help me organize the attic."

"I'd even do that to get a few minutes in that room. But if the ghost is really Amalie and your aunt doesn't know she's there, don't you think you ought to tell her?"

Drew remembered the look on Aunt Jocelyn's face when she'd asked who Amalie was. She thought about how guilty her aunt must have felt all these years, feeling that she'd been the cause of her death—and Evan's. And Aunt Jocelyn had already said she didn't believe in ghosts. "No. Not yet, anyway." She shifted gears as they began a long upward incline.

"I guess it makes sense to wait till we're really sure."

"Don't forget, you might not be able to get into that room at all," Drew said, standing up to pedal harder, her legs straining. "I couldn't get the door open before."

They rode without talking to conserve their breath until they'd reached the top and shifted gears again.

Will let go of his handlebars then and crossed his arms over his chest as they began to gather speed on the downward slope. "Where there's a Will, there's a way!"

As Drew groaned, he leaned forward and took the handlebars again, pedaling to speed ahead of her.

Aunt Jocelyn readily agreed to let Will come help Drew in the attic. "It's long past time we got some order up there," she said. "But you'd better plan to work early in the morning or it'll be too hot to do anything. It'll take some time. When do you want to start?"

"How about tomorrow?" Somehow the thought of a ghost in that room had become even more unsettling now that the ghost had a name and a story. If Will was going to try communicating with her, the sooner the better. He'd told Drew that once a ghost accomplishes whatever task has kept it haunting, it goes away. The sooner the better, definitely.

"Tomorrow's fine," Aunt Jocelyn said.

Drew called Will after dinner. His voice was exuberant when he promised to be there by eight o'clock the next morning.

When the dishes were done, Drew offered to read to her grandfather so her aunt could take a little break. She dreaded the thought of the hot, dim room, the difficult old man, but she kept remembering what Mrs. Connelly had said about Jocelyn's wasted life. Aunt Jocelyn shook her head. "It's kind of you to offer, but he's used to me. He doesn't cope with str—change very well." She was going to say *strangers,* Drew thought. *She* doesn't think of us that way anymore, even if Grandfather does.

Drew went up to her room to read the rest of Amalie's poetry. Evan had closed himself and Pandora into his room again.

She opened the book and looked at the photo. Amalie was smiling a soft half smile. Drew could believe that the people of Riverton were bowled over by Amalie Broderick.

There was a foreword to the book, written by Gilbert Broderick, explaining that the volume had been published posthumously as a memorial to the poet, his beloved wife, who had given her life in a tragically futile attempt to save the stepson she had so lovingly taken to her heart.

He went on to explain that most of the poems had been composed in his wife's writing room, where she worked at the window overlooking the rose garden, which included several special hybrid roses that had been planted as a wedding present to her. "She called the garden 'her muse,' and she became so devoted to roses that she wore only Rose Petal perfume. These poems celebrate roses and beauty, love and life, as did their creator."

Roses and beauty and life, perhaps, Drew thought, as she closed the book some time later, but not poetry. She felt as if she'd just read her way through an entire greeting-card store. And then she wished she could apologize to the poet. Amalie must have believed the sugary sentiments in the poems and worked hard to keep the so-careful rhythm, the steady rhyme.

The sun had gone down and the breeze was chilly. Drew got up to close her window and heard again the soft singing coming from Evan's room. He'll be talking soon, she thought. There's something about this place that's changing him. Healing him.

She stood for a moment, looking out at the slope of green softening to gray in the evening shadows. She thought of how she was beginning to feel about Aunt Jocelyn, about Will. Was it doing the same for her?

"Do you think your aunt would mind?" Will said the next morning as they stood in the hall outside the writing room door.

Drew shrugged. "It isn't as if you're going to *do* anything; I can't imagine it would be a problem just to go in. Besides, she won't know. She went into town for groceries. Evan's downstairs with Pandora listening for the bell, and he's to come get me if Grandfather rings." Then she remembered. "I left this door unlatched before."

"It's closed now." Will reached out and took hold of the doorknob. Drew held her breath. He turned it, the latch clicked, and the door swung open. "So much for not being able to get in," he said, and walked in. "You coming?"

Drew hesitated, peering past him into what looked like a perfectly ordinary, even charming, little room.

"Come on. It's empty. And not even chilly."

Though the shade was firmly down, the room was surprisingly light, brightened by the pale yellow wallpaper sprigged with white rosebuds. Drapes of fabric with the same print framed the window, in front of which stood an antique writing desk and a small chair with a green velvet seat and back. Prints of old-fashioned roses with names like Maiden's Blush and La France hung on the walls above glass-fronted bookcases. Everything in the room was covered with a fine layer of dust, and there was a musty, faintly mildewy smell. Fine gray lines of cobwebs stretched from the cream-colored shades of two ornate gold wall lamps to the ceiling.

Will stood in the center of the room and turned slowly all the way around. "No ghost," he said.

Drew felt oddly disappointed. Relieved, but disappointed, too. "No cold, either." In fact, it was hot and stuffy.

"Rats!" Will said. "I really wanted to meet her."

Drew looked at the soft gold of the Oriental rug, with its pattern of birds and flowers. It was a room that would have encouraged poetry even in someone who wasn't a poetic genius. "She must have sat there at the desk, writing and looking out over the rose garden." Drew had a sudden realization. *"That's* why there are no roses at Rose Hill. Amalie loved them so much that after she died, Grandfather couldn't stand to look at them anymore. So he had them all torn out."

Will had opened the top drawer of the desk, revealing a pad of yellowing paper and a green, marbleized fountain pen. He turned to look at Drew. "Did your aunt tell you that?"

"She didn't have to. I just know. It's hard to have something around that keeps reminding you over and over of somebody you'll never see again."

Will's face changed suddenly and he closed the desk drawer. "I'm sorry! I haven't even been thinking about what you and Evan... All this stuff about ghosts, death. I shouldn't have—I'm sorry."

"That's all right. Mostly, I'd rather have people forget. It's easier." Maybe it was the relief of being in this room she had been avoiding, and finding it just an ordinary room. Or maybe it was the look of genuine concern on Will's face. But suddenly, and for the very first time, she felt like talking. "It was hard to be around the kids at school after the accident, all of them being so careful, never knowing what to say to me or how to treat me. It was like there was this glass bubble around me, keeping me in and everybody else out. We could see each other, but that was all. We couldn't touch. It wasn't my friends' fault. It wasn't anybody's fault. I think they were scared. Because I was just one of them and then all of a sudden, on a perfectly ordinary day, I came to school like every other day and there was that gas leak and our house blew up and both of my parents were gone. Like it could happen to anybody at all, anytime. It could happen to any of them."

Will reached out to touch her shoulder, a sort of clumsy pat. "It must have been awful."

Drew nodded. "I was glad to get away when school was out. Because somehow the things my friends were interested in didn't seem all that important to me anymore. They'd been important before, but everything—*everything*—had changed. And I was glad to get away from that town, where so much reminded me of my mother and father and the way things had been. That's how I knew about the roses. Grandfather wrote about them in the front of Amalie's book of poems. I'm just sure that when Amalie was gone, he never wanted to see another rose again. They reminded him, and he couldn't bear to remember." She paused. She understood exactly. "He couldn't bear to remember."

"So why didn't he change this room, I wonder."

"Maybe he just never came back up here. Aunt Jocelyn said the upstairs hasn't been lived in for thirty years. Maybe from the day they found the bodies, he never came back to the bedroom he had shared with her, never came to her writing room."

Will hit his forehead with the palm of one hand. "Maybe that's it! That's why she still comes back here. She wants to tell him to stop grieving for her. She wouldn't want him to have spent all these years in so much pain. She waits for him to come back to this room, but he never does."

Drew thought about that and then shook her head slowly. "She loved him so much, and they'd only been married for a year or so. Maybe it's just that she couldn't leave him. Maybe she's been waiting for him. If that's it, and if Grandfather is as sick as I think he is, she won't have to wait very much longer. When he dies, they'll be together and she'll finally be able to go—with him."

"I thought you said you don't read romance novels."

"I don't."

"A haunting for a great love." Will stooped to look at the books in one of the bookcases. "Huhn! You're probably right. Half the books in here are collections of love poetry."

Drew moved past him to the desk. "Anyway, we don't know for sure that she's haunting at all. She isn't here now. We know that!"

She leaned over the desk. "I wonder how the rose garden looked from up here." She reached out to push the curtain out of the way and raise the shade. And felt a cold draft across her hand.

The room, which had been hot, began to feel chilly, and then, so fast that Drew felt the skin on her arms and neck break into goose bumps, it was cold. A deep, bone-chilling cold. She gasped with the shock of the sudden change and noticed a sweet scent on the air. "Roses," she managed to say, turning to Will.

His body was rigid, his eyes staring at something over her left shoulder. The scent of roses grew heavier. Slowly, reluctantly, she turned to look where Will was looking. There, in front of the curtain, she saw what seemed to be a column of smoke turning in the still air like a dust devil, forming itself into a shape. She stepped back, her stomach lurching.

"Amalie?" she heard Will asking. "Amalie Broderick? Is that you?"

Feeling as if she was about to faint, Drew flung herself at Will and grabbed his arm, dragging him toward the door. Her teeth were chattering now in the cold. She would not, could not turn back to the window. She didn't think she could stand to see the shape that would be coming clearer behind her, the shape that she could feel moving toward her.

"No, Drew," Will was saying, trying to dislodge her hands from his arm. "We have to stay...."

But Drew could not. If she didn't get out of the cold, out of the room, away from that scent right this minute, she was going to be sick.

In a moment, she found herself in the warm hall, holding on to the stairwell rail with all her strength. Will was at the writing room door, which had slammed shut behind them, pushing at it with both hands.

"I can't open it," he said. "It's stuck again."

Drew felt cold air from under the door drift across her sandaled feet.

FOURTEEN

DREW AND WILL sat at the kitchen table and sipped the lemon tea Drew had made. Evan had been there with Pandora when they came down, but they'd sent him outdoors, telling him they'd listen for Grandfather's bell.

"You shouldn't have dragged me out," Will was saying. "She was trying to materialize, and she was just beginning to be recognizable. I could see her hair and the flowers on her dress. If we'd waited, I might have been able to ask her why she's still here."

Drew, her hands still shaky, held tightly to the hot mug. "I couldn't stay there. And I didn't want you to stay, either. Didn't you feel it? The cold? That sickening sweet smell? Something really evil was happening, Will. Something dangerous."

"It wasn't evil. She can't have changed from a good live person to an evil ghost."

Drew shuddered. In spite of the hot, sweet tea, her stomach had not quite settled. "But the cold—"

"I've read about that. In order to materialize, to be seen by living people, a ghost has to use a huge amount of energy. Some people think it takes that energy in the form of heat from its surroundings. She can't help it. She didn't mean to frighten us; she just wanted us to be able to see her."

"I don't want to see her."

"But I'll bet you wouldn't be as frightened if you could. I mean, if she managed to materialize completely, she'd look just the way she looked when I saw her in the window, like a person. She'd look like her photograph. And you couldn't be afraid of that woman, could you? At least you couldn't if you didn't keep reminding yourself that she's a ghost. It's really only the idea of it that's scaring you."

Drew sipped her tea and then set her mug

down on the table to still her shaking hands. "All I know is that I've never been so frightened in my life. And it felt as if there was something to be frightened of. It did! It wasn't just the cold or the rose smell or the sick feeling it gave me—" Drew stopped. "The sick feeling! I had it up in the attic that first time I went up there exploring. And then again when I tried to open the writing room door. And both times there was that same sweet smell. Rose Petal perfume!"

"Maybe she was trying to appear to you."

Drew tried to remember exactly what she'd been doing in the attic when she'd first felt sick. She'd found the rabbit that time and set it next to Lulu. But when had the sick feeling come? When the smell came, of course. When she'd opened that box with the letters. She'd thought it was perfumed stationery. If the smell had meant that Amalie was there, it might not have been connected to those letters at all. "There wasn't that awful cold, but maybe that's because she wasn't trying to materialize. She was just there. I'd found Bunn." She thought about that. "Will! I had just found Bunn!"

"So?"

Drew remembered Evan's reaction when she

had asked him about going to the attic and taking Bunn. He had made it clear he hadn't been in the attic. And she'd been so sure he was lying. She hadn't thought to wonder *why* he would lie. Maybe it wasn't a lie at all. Maybe Bunn really had just turned up in his room. "Do you think Amalie could have taken Bunn to Evan? Left it in his room while he was sleeping?"

Will shrugged. "Could be, I guess." He snapped his fingers. "I bet that's it. Evan is just about the age the first Evan was when he drowned, isn't he?"

"A couple of years older."

"Close enough. Amalie probably still feels bad that she couldn't save him, and for some reason she hasn't gone on to wherever she was supposed to go after she died. Suddenly, your Evan is here, maybe reminding her. He's little and he's sad, just the way the other Evan was when she began taking care of him. It would be natural for her to want to take care of this one. One way to do that would be to give him the first Evan's favorite stuffed animal for comfort."

Drew remembered suddenly the singing from Evan's room. It had been a song she didn't know. And the voice had been too soft, almost a whispery singing, to recognize. What if it wasn't Evan singing to himself at all? What if—no, it couldn't have been. "Do you suppose a ghost could sing?"

Will shrugged. "Sing or talk or carry rabbits— I don't know what ghosts can do! If they can wail and cry, I guess they could sing. Why? Have you heard singing from the writing room?"

"From Evan's room. I thought it was Evan. But I didn't know the song, and the voice was too low and quiet to recognize. I suppose it could have been a woman's voice instead of a child's. I first heard it a couple of nights ago, and then just the other evening."

"So—she brings Evan the first Evan's rabbit. And then goes to his room, maybe, to sing him to sleep. You did say that he seems better since he's been here."

"Yes, but part of what I thought was better was his singing. I thought he was trying out his voice by himself in his own room and might be getting ready to talk in public, too."

Will leaned back in his chair. "Do you mean you think he's been faking it and he really could talk if he wanted to? Is that what the doctor told you?"

Drew shook her head. "I'm the only one who

thought that. I couldn't believe a person could suddenly not be able to talk—not someone who used to talk as much as Evan. It isn't that I didn't think it was caused by grief, only that I thought his grief made him not *want* to talk. And when I heard the singing, it seemed to prove it. That after the accident he just didn't want to talk anymore, and that maybe he liked the attention it got him not to talk. Here, where he didn't get so much attention for that, I thought he was beginning to get ready to talk again."

"Does he seem better, though, otherwise?"

Drew nodded. "He is better. Something good has been happening for him here."

"So?" Will drained his mug. "Seems to me that just about proves it. Amalie goes to him at night and sings to him and comforts him, just like a mother would. Just like she used to do with Evan one."

A flash of memory hit Drew so fast that she didn't have time to block it out. Herself, snuggled into bed, her rainbow night-light on, and her mother sitting by her bed, her chestnut curls caught at the nape of her neck with a tortoiseshell barrette, her long, slim fingers plucking guitar strings, singing. The song was suddenly in her mind, filling it with her mother's voice and the sound of quiet chords: *Wynken, Blynken, and Nod one night/Sailed off in a wooden shoe—/Sailed on a river of crystal light....* Her eyes were suddenly swimming with tears. She rubbed her hand across them and took a sip of her rapidly cooling tea.

"Are you okay?" Will asked. "What—?"

"I'm fine," Drew managed to say. "Just remembered something, that's all." That's why she didn't ever let the memories in. That's why. She forced the images away, replacing them with the memory of that terrible cold, the sick-sweet scent of roses. "How could Evan be comforted by that cold? That rose smell? I don't understand."

"Probably Amalie only makes that terrible cold when she's trying to become visible. By the time she comes out of that room and all the way down the hall to where Evan is, the cold is probably gone and she's just a woman wanting to comfort a grieving child."

"What about me?" Drew asked. "Why doesn't she want to comfort me?"

Will looked at her, his eyes cool and appraising. "You're the same age your aunt was when the tragedy happened, aren't you?"

"Almost."

"So what if you remind her of Jocelyn? She might blame Jocelyn for her death, remember— and Evan's."

Drew nodded. "But what about Pandora?" she asked. "You said animals are a sure giveaway. And Pandora won't go near the writing room. But she spends the night in Evan's room every night. She's been in there with him whenever I've heard the singing."

Will rubbed his cheek, frowning. "That's a tough one. Maybe the only thing that bothered Pandora is what bothers you—the cold. And that just happens in the writing room."

"Maybe."

As she and Will went up to the attic to do some of the work they were supposed to be doing this morning, Drew could not stop the fear. Even if the cold really was no more than Amalie trying to make herself visible, it scared her more than anything had scared her ever in her life.

In the afternoon, Drew helped hang her grandfather's freshly washed bedding on a clothesline. "There's nothing like the sun to get rid of a sickroom smell," Aunt Jocelyn said.

Afterward, they went in for lemonade.

"So," Jocelyn said when they'd sat down at the kitchen table, "did you and Will get much accomplished in the attic this morning?"

Drew shook her head. "Mostly we just moved furniture and boxes so you can get around up there more easily."

"I should call an antique dealer and see if there's anything up there worth selling."

"When you were cleaning upstairs before Evan and I came, did you notice any-thing...strange...near the writing room?" Drew found herself holding her breath as she waited for the answer.

Aunt Jocelyn frowned. "I only cleaned the rooms you were going to be using. What do you mean 'strange'?"

"A smell. Or cold."

Jocelyn laughed a short laugh that was almost more like a cough. "Cold has never been a problem during the summer. We used to sleep out on the lawn sometimes when we were kids because it got so hot. Why?"

How could she put this? Drew wondered. "There's something weird up there. I think—" There seemed to be no way except just to say it. "I think there's a ghost. I think it's Amalie Broderick."

Jocelyn set her glass down. "That's the most ridiculous thing I ever heard."

"Will's seen her," Drew said. "He says she looks exactly like the picture in her book of poetry."

Jocelyn, her face set, shook her head. "An overactive imagination. I suppose you've seen this apparition as well?"

"No. Only a sort of mist—but I've felt the cold she makes and smelled her rose perfume. Have you been in the writing room lately?"

Another shake of the head. "I don't go there. We've had people come in to clean up there once a year...." She paused, frowning. "A woman I hired to wash windows one time quit halfway through the job. She wouldn't give me any reason." She picked up her glass again and drained it. "That doesn't mean there's a ghost."

"When was the last time you were in the writing room?"

Jocelyn looked into her empty glass for a moment before answering. "Probably the last time was the week of Amalie's funeral. Father asked me to pack up her things. I started, but I couldn't bear to touch them. So your father did it for me. I could never face going back."

"Will and I think she's there. She must be staying for a reason. Maybe she has a message for you. Or for Grandfather."

Aunt Jocelyn turned on Drew, her eyes so intense Drew had to look away. "I don't want to hear another word about Amalie. Ever! That's past and gone—and ought to be forgotten. If there's a heaven—and I fervently hope there is— Amalie Broderick is there with my brother Evan. They're waiting for Father to come and join them. She is not stuck here like some demon"— Jocelyn shuddered—"haunting this house! You haven't mentioned this theory of yours to your brother, I hope."

"No," Drew said, focusing on the little pool of water her lemonade glass had made on the table.

"Don't. I'm sorry if the shock of your own loss has given you these crazy ideas. But there will be no more talk of ghosts in this house! I don't want to hear any more about ghosts! Do you hear me? No more talk of ghosts!" Jocelyn stood up then and took her glass to the sink. "I must go check on Father."

Left alone at the table, Drew was suddenly

swept with sympathy for the ghost of Amalie Broderick. She imagined her wanting desperately to communicate something, waiting all alone through the long years in a deserted part of the house with no one coming near except an occasional housekeeper or a terrified window washer. Then, when she finally had a chance to connect with someone, the very effort to do it created that terrifying cold.

Drew was glad Amalie had Evan, at least, who didn't get sick with fear. But whatever her message, Evan, unable or unwilling to speak, could not deliver it. And Aunt Jocelyn wouldn't believe that Amalie was there at all.

CHAPTER
FIFTEEN

WHEN JOCELYN TOOK her father's dinner tray to him that evening, she came back to the kitchen a few moments later, her face as pale as skim milk. "He's so deeply asleep, I can't wake him," she said, reaching for the phone to call his doctor. Drew, setting the table, heard the word *coma* and did her best to close her mind to it. Was there going to be more death?

"Dr. Merriam will come by after his hospital rounds," Aunt Jocelyn said when she hung up. "I'm going to stay with Father till he comes. Dinner's done—you just have to serve it."

After dinner, Drew and Evan rinsed the dishes

and put them into the dishwasher. Pandora would not settle, but kept rubbing against their legs, so constantly present that Drew nearly fell over her twice. Finally, she sent both Evan and the cat out with the warning that they were to go no farther than the carriage house. Evan, his forehead creased with worry, picked up his cat, rubbed his cheek against her ears, and went. As Drew watched Evan trudge along the flagstones toward the lily garden, Pandora winding in and out between his legs, she wondered what another death, if it happened now, might do to the beginnings of his recovery.

If Amalie were here not to give someone a message but only waiting for her husband to join her, would his death take both of them away? She felt a twinge of guilt. It wasn't that she wanted her grandfather to die, she told herself, only that Amalie's leaving would mean the cold would go, and the scent of roses, and her own terror.

But by the time the doctor arrived, Gilbert Broderick was not only awake; he was strong enough to make his voice heard through his closed door in protest. "Can't a man take a nap without having his home invaded by strangers?"

Drew heard Aunt Jocelyn's protest that it wasn't just a nap and Dr. Merriam was hardly a stranger. She started upstairs. Darkness was still a long way away. If Amalie was going to stay in this house, then Drew had to find a way to overcome her fear, maybe even, as Will said, try to communicate with her.

She remembered the wave of sympathy she'd felt for Amalie. Now, with Evan outside, Jocelyn busy with Grandfather and the doctor, and the sun still lighting everything with a warm, ruddy glow, maybe she could brave the writing room. Amalie alive had been nothing to fear. And Amalie even now seemed able to comfort Evan.

Whatever her reason for being so afraid, Drew had to overcome that fear. How else could she stay in this house? She would go into the writing room, pull up the shade to let in the light, and wait. Maybe Amalie, on the other side of the blank and terrible reality of death, could find a way to communicate. Maybe she could comfort her as she comforted Evan.

Drew felt the smooth wood of the stair railing under her hand as she climbed the stairs. How often, she wondered, had Amalie climbed these stairs, her hand on this same railing? *I'm coming,*

Drew thought. *I'm coming. You can talk to me.* And then, quite suddenly, Drew felt the hair on the back of her neck rising. Climbing the stairs this way, as she came up to the level of the second floor, the writing room was directly behind her. Was she imagining the feel of cold at her back?

An image rose in her mind of cold air, like a thin line of fog, pouring out from under the writing room door, across the hall, through the stairwell railing, and down over her head and shoulders and down her back. She stopped. Her hands began to tremble and she turned and hurried down the stairs, trying not to imagine the cold coming after her.

That night, she had the dream again. Again she was running, her feet mired in something heavy, sticky. A smell of mud, of rot and decay, rose around her, and whatever was coming from behind closed in, this time bringing with it cold. A terrible bone-shattering cold. Then, over the stench of rot, layering it, obliterating it, came the sweet smell of roses.

Drew woke, clutching her sheet to her chest. Only a dream, she told herself. Only a dream. But she was still shivering, still so cold she could hardly move. Her teeth were chattering so she could hear the sound, loud against the silence of the house. She grabbed for Lulu and held her tight. And then she noticed the smell: roses. Her room was filled with the heavy sweetness of roses. Quickly, she turned on the light next to her bed.

The room filled with the comforting glow that pushed back shadows. But it did not push back the cold or the smell of roses. Drew lay there for a moment, her teeth still chattering, telling herself she was imagining it. This was nothing but residue from the dream. But then she noticed her breath. In the light of the lamp, her breath made little puffs of grayish white mist. The cold was real, as real as going outside on a winter morning.

"Amalie," she quavered, trying to steady her voice. "Is that you, Amalie?" No sound, no change. Only the pale puffs of her breath and the heavy, sweet smell. Amalie was a loving person, she told herself. The cold is only from trying to materialize. There is nothing evil about it. "Amalie? I want to help you."

Nothing. Drew dragged her bedspread up and huddled under it, hoping to get warmer, but if anything changed, it was getting colder. Finally, gritting her teeth, she threw off the covers and, still clutching Lulu, got out of bed. She stood for a moment at the door, shivering, afraid to open it, afraid of what she might see on the other side.

"One, two, three!" she said aloud, and threw open the door. There was nothing but darkness. She turned away from the old house, hurried down the dark hall, and plunged down the back stairs, not stopping until she was pounding on Aunt Jocelyn's bedroom door.

"What is it?" Jocelyn said when she finally opened the door, a robe clutched around her shoulders. "What's the matter?"

"I...I need a qu-quilt," Drew said. "Or a blanket. Something. I'm c-c-cold!" Her teeth had begun chattering again.

"Cold? Just a moment." Aunt Jocelyn disappeared and was back in a moment with a folded comforter. "This ought to be more than enough. And for heaven's sake, close your window," she said.

Drew didn't tell her that the window wasn't open. She just took the comforter and went back to the bottom of the back stairs. Would her room have returned to normal when she got back? she wondered. Did she dare go back? She flipped the light switch so that the stairs and the upper hall were filled with light. It wasn't enough to make the fear go away, but it helped.

Back in her room, she saw that her breath no longer puffed visibly on the air. But it was still cold, the smell of roses like a shadow on the air. She checked the window again just to be certain. Closed.

She left the light on and climbed back into bed, pulling the comforter up over her head so that there was only the tiniest air hole, and waited for warmth to come back and her shivering to stop. "I wish I could talk to Will," she whispered to the smudged, smiling face of the one-armed doll. "I just wish I could talk to Will." Maybe the cold *wasn't* just Amalie's attempt to become visible. Maybe it was something else.

If Amalie could be warm and loving to Evan, why did she always bring such cold to Drew? Had she mistaken her for Jocelyn? Did she blame her for the death of Evan one?

The thought was too terrible. How could she go on living here? But there was nowhere else in the world for her except with the Tildens. She could not go back to the Tildens. Besides, Rose

Hill was home. She had as much right to be here as Amalie Broderick, and she hadn't done anything wrong.

Drew lifted the comforter for a moment and took a long breath of the still-cold air. Somehow she would have to find out why Amalie was here and how to get her to go. Somehow.

CHAPTER
SIXTEEN

SWEAT STREAMING DOWN her face, Drew dragged at boxes, moving what she and Will had moved the day before. It was only a little after ten, but already the attic was oppressive, the sun beating down on the roof. She didn't mind the heat so much, she told herself, when she remembered last night.

At breakfast, she had longed to tell Aunt Jocelyn what had happened in her room. But even if she didn't mention the word *ghost*, she knew what the reaction would be. Bad dream. Then, as she was taking a bite of toast, she'd suddenly remembered something. The first time she'd smelled Amalie's perfume and felt the nausea that it caused, she'd been opening the box marked with a black letter *A*. *A* for Amalie. It had been Amalie's things she'd been looking at. Maybe somewhere in that box, in those letters, was a clue to Amalie's staying. It hadn't been Bunn that Amalie had come for. She'd been trying, as best she could, to communicate something, and Drew had not understood.

So now she was looking for that box, cursing herself and Will for having invented the cleanup story as a way to get Will into the house. Because they really *had* done some organizing—enough so that now she had no idea where that box had gotten to. They had carefully pushed furniture to one side of the attic, stacked boxes on the other side, newer boxes in the new part of the house, old ones in the old. But there were so many and they looked so much alike. She remembered exactly where it had been before. Why couldn't they have left well enough alone?

Drew lifted a box off the top of a stack she had newly uncovered, and there it was. The black *A* with a circle around it. Amalie's box. Wiping her forehead with her arm to keep the sweat from dripping into her eyes, she lifted the box and carried it to a spot she'd cleared directly under the bare overhead lightbulb. She set it on the floor and squatted next to it. For a moment, she only sat there, looking at the folded-in flaps of ordinary brown cardboard, the circled *A*. It was her father who had cleaned out the writing room. He must have written that *A*, circled it. She traced the letter with one finger. Then she took a deep breath and pulled back the flaps. The letters were jumbled against one side, papers and cards and the edges of legal pads showing beneath.

She reached in and took out the letters, aware as she did so that the heat around her seemed less noticeable. She did her best to ignore that and opened the first envelope to take out a letter written in flowing letters with turquoise ink on pink stationery. It was dated January 1961. "Amalie, dearest," it began. Drew checked the last page. It was signed, "Love and roses, Dorothy." She skimmed the letter quickly, trying not to focus on the chill that was growing around her. "I'm doing my best," she muttered. "Just let me look. You don't have to be here."

There was nothing in this letter. Just some mean gossip about some people named Ross and Elsie that Amalie and Dorothy had known in college. Drew put the letter back into the envelope and opened another.

This one, with the same greeting, was dated April 1961. After a few lines about the weather, its breezy tone changed. "Kittery is the right place for Jocelyn," she read. "So stick to your guns. Boarding school's a perfectly normal thing for a rich kid. Besides, you have the perfect excuse. Everyone's heard of Kittery's art department. Don't let that fool Broderick back out on the idea the way he did with the little one." Drew stopped and reread the line. "That fool Broderick." Was this Dorothy person talking about her grandfather? The love of Amalie's life?

She read on. "Imagine the next four years with a teenager underfoot. Bad enough you're going to have that little brat to deal with till you can figure out something else. You can hire somebody to take care of him, of course, except it'll make a dent in your image. I shudder to think what the next twelve years will be like if you can't do anything without having to worry about the poor motherless tot. At least the oldest one's out and gone. I warned you about ready-made families, if you'll remember. You've worked so hard to make a place for yourself there, Grand Lady of the Manor and all, you can't waste your life playing nursemaid and mommy to somebody else's kid."

Drew realized the paper was moving as she read it. The cold had grown so that her hands were shaking. "That little brat." Evan? Kittery must have been the art school Aunt Jocelyn was supposed to go to. Not to develop her talent, as everybody said—as Amalie had said—but to get her out of the house. Drew looked at the post-mark on the envelope. Dorothy had written from California. Mrs. Connelly had said Gilbert Brod-erick met Amalie out west when he was away on a business trip. California?

If Amalie was the person everyone in Riv-erton thought she was, how could an old friend write such things to her? Dorothy wasn't invent-ing anything in this letter; she had to be respond-ing to what Amalie had told her. There was no other explanation, Drew realized. Except that the generous, loving, artistic Amalie had to have been a fraud.

She dropped the letter on the floor and snatched the next one out of its envelope. This one was dated February. She skimmed it quickly, aware of the scent of roses growing around her with the cold. Nothing. More nasty gossip.

There was one more envelope. She opened the letter it contained. This one was dated August

20, 1961, and it began without the usual prelim-
inaries. "Amalie, you idiot, you mentioned your
journal. You haven't been recording all this, have
you?" All what? Drew wondered. "I'd have
thought you learned your lesson our junior year.
Anyway, that was only kid stuff. This is different.
It isn't enough to find a good safe hiding place.
You should never have written it down at all.
And don't give me that crap about the 'soul of
the poet.' This is too serious. You could lose
everything. EVERYTHING! Listen to Darling
Dorothy—put this letter down right now—
RIGHT NOW!!—and go burn that journal!!!!" It
was signed only with a big looping *D*.

Drew sat back on her heels. The attic had
gone from sweltering to freezing, and the smell
of roses was so strong, she could hardly take
a breath without gagging. August. Evan and
Amalie had died in August. What had Amalie's
journal contained that could have lost her everything? Had she done what Dorothy told her to
do? Had she burned it?

Drew's breath was coming in short gasps. She
noticed she could see them now, puffs hovering
for brief moments in the air in front of her
mouth. She closed her eyes for a moment, swal-

lowed hard, willing her heart to slow down, her hands to stop shaking, and then gathered the letters and jammed them into the waistband of her shorts, under her T-shirt. Hurriedly, she dumped the contents of the cardboard box on the floor at her feet. Papers, envelopes, and notebooks scattered, sliding over one another. She sorted through them, scattering them further.

A journal, Dorothy had said. From what little she knew of Amalie, she didn't think she'd have done such writing on a plain tablet or in a spiral-bound notebook. She would have had something far more elegant, like the one in which she'd written her poetry. There was nothing like that in this box. And she had seen no other box marked with an *A*.

The cold was so bad now that Drew couldn't concentrate anymore. She pushed herself to her feet, her fingers numb. At the top of the stairs, she thought she could see the beginnings of that column of swirling mist. Drew clenched her fists, held her breath, and flung herself past it and onto the stairs. She pounded down them, slipping near the bottom and crashing into the closed door. Near panic, she wrenched it open and was out into the hot, still, bright hall.

Her heart felt as if it would pop out of her

chest. She forced herself to slow down and walked as quietly as possible down the back stairs and through the kitchen.

"Drew?" Aunt Jocelyn said, looking up from something she was stirring on the stove. "What's the matter? Drew?"

But Drew didn't answer. And she didn't stop until she was in the old greenhouse, sitting in the hot, still, blinding, blessed sunlight.

She took the letters out and stared at them. She would have to show them to Aunt Jocelyn, she knew that. But she wanted Will to see them first. Then he could go with her when she did. But Will was in Albany at the orthodontist. So she could do nothing until tomorrow.

Drew had to find the journal, if it still existed. It was her father who had cleaned out the writing room. And her father had been the only one who had not loved Amalie. Had he found Dorothy's letters, too? Is that what the final argument had been about? Had he tried to tell his father the truth about the wonderful, beloved Amalie?

Drew pushed her dresser against her closed door when she went to bed that night, hoping that somehow what she'd heard about ghosts going through doors and walls couldn't be true. She had surprised Evan by going to his room to tuck him in, being sure Pandora was snuggled down against his legs before she left. The new Amalie, Dorothy's Amalie, didn't fit the image of comforter of small boys. Drew didn't understand about the singing, about the rabbit, but she was glad Evan had Pandora with him. She had a feeling that the cat would know if he was in any kind of danger.

She folded the letters carefully and slipped them under her mattress before crawling into bed. And she didn't turn off her light. Though it was very warm in her room, she covered herself clear to her nose with the comforter. Feeling sweaty and vaguely silly, she cradled Lulu against her chest.

Tomorrow, she could get Will to help her find that journal and go with her to talk to Aunt Jocelyn. She wasn't sure what her aunt could do, but somehow she needed her to know what was happening, to *know* that Rose Hill was haunted and that Amalie hadn't been the person everyone thought.

Drew awoke with a sudden jolt. The room was freezing, the smell of roses heavy in the air.

She jerked the comforter up over her head and squeezed her eyes shut so she wouldn't see that column of swirling mist again. She lay for a moment trying to think what to do. The dresser was against the door, so it wouldn't be easy to get up and out. But how could she stay in the room?

She couldn't. Taking a deep breath of the warmer air under the comforter and keeping her eyes shut, she threw back the covers. Lulu fell to the floor and Drew stepped on the rag body as she got up. She opened her eyes. And Amalie was there, standing between the window and the end of her bed, her flowery dress clear, her long blond hair the color of honey, her face the face from the photograph, perfect in every detail. Drew might have thought her a real person except that she seemed to float in the air, not quite solidly connected to the floor. And her eyes seemed to burn with pure hatred. There was no mistaking that expression.

Drew's breath caught in her throat as Amalie began to move toward her. The legs and arms didn't seem to be moving, and yet the whole image was getting closer, larger.

Drew ran for the door and shoved the dresser out of the way. Fear had grown in her mind so that it blotted everything else out except the need to run, to get away—from this ghost, this room, this house.

She jerked at the door. It crashed into the dresser; she hadn't moved it far enough. She could feel Amalie coming closer. She squeezed through the crack between dresser and door and slammed her hand against the switch on the wall, flooding the hall with light. She caught a glimpse of Evan's door, cracked open slightly. Pandora's head emerged and Drew turned and fled down the long front staircase. The sound of the cat yowling, the horrifying scream of that first day, filled Drew's head until she thought it might burst her skull.

It was exactly like the dream, the evil closing in behind her, the need to run propelling her forward. The front door was closed. She twisted the knob. Closed and locked. Feeling Amalie coming closer, she scrabbled at the dead bolt. It wouldn't give. Still the cat yowled from above.

Drew turned and looked back up the stairs. Amalie had stopped halfway down the stairs. Above her, *through* her, Drew could see Evan in his pajamas, his eyes wide, the stuffed rabbit clutched against his chest. Pandora, back arched, tail puffed, was backed against the wall behind him, still yowling.

And Amalie vanished. One moment she was there, turned halfway to look from Evan to Drew, and then she was gone.

Evan stood for a moment, looking down. And then, slowly, Pandora moved forward until she stood next to him, rubbing her cheek gently against his pale, thin leg.

"What in thunderation is going on out there?" came their grandfather's voice.

"Drew? Evan?" And Aunt Jocelyn was there. "Whatever is the matter with Pandora?"

CHAPTER
SEVENTEEN

"I THINK SHE saw a mouse," Drew said to Aunt Jocelyn, who had come hurrying from her room in her nightgown without even taking time to grab her robe.

"That must have been some mouse," Aunt Jocelyn said, looking up to where Evan was crouched, petting Pandora. Drew thought she would have said more, would have come upstairs to investigate, but Grandfather's querulous voice drew her instead back down the hall to his room.

"I'll see that Evan gets back to bed," she called after her aunt's retreating back. "Don't worry about us."

Evan's eyes were wide, his teeth chattering. But he seemed more concerned for Pandora than frightened. She wished she could say the same for herself. It was all she could do to go back up those stairs, aware every second that the writing room was behind her and that wherever Amalie had gone when she vanished, she was somewhere on the second floor of that house, hating her. *Hating me,* she thought over and over as she took each step upward.

I'd probably be in another county by now if I'd been able to get the door open, she thought as she reached the top of the stairs. Evan, clutching Bunn in one arm, reached out and touched Drew's arm with his free hand. He looked up into her eyes, his forehead creased. She knew he was trying to communicate something, but she couldn't tell what it was. Pandora moved from his legs to Drew's, winding in and out between the two of them, arching her back as she rubbed against them, her tail wrapping around first one and then the other.

Evan took Drew's hand then and pulled her toward his room. "It's okay," she told him, going along, trying not to trip over the cat. "She was after me, not you."

Evan nodded vigorously, as if he'd already

known that, and led her after him through his doorway. In his room, the elephant lamp glowed, casting a soft, comforting light. There was no chill, no hint of rose scent. Drew's heart had slowed its frantic thumping and she was breathing evenly again. She closed the door carefully behind them, listening for the click of the latch. Evan stopped at the rocking chair for a moment. Pandora rubbed her cheek against the nearest rocker and set the chair in motion.

Then Evan climbed onto his bed, sat cross-legged, still clutching Bunn, and patted the mattress next to him.

"Okay," Drew said. "I'll stay for a bit and watch out for you."

But oddly, from the moment they had come through the doorway into his room, it seemed almost the other way around. The room felt warm without being stuffy—warm and still and safe—as if the cold, hating Amalie would not come in here. That was because of Evan, of course. Drew was the one Amalie hated, not Evan. But what if Amalie came after her in here? She made a movement as if to get up and Evan put his hand on her arm.

"Okay," she said again. "All right. You win.

I'm here for the night." And she was suddenly glad, for herself as much as for him. She rubbed her hand through Evan's hair, smoothing it. He grinned up at her, the elfin grin, and turned so that she could rub his head. It was something she had begun doing when he was scarcely more than a baby, pushing his curls up from his neck to the top of his head, then back down again, over and over. He'd always loved it.

Suddenly, feeling the soft silkiness of his hair between her fingers, remembering all the other times, she realized she hadn't done this since their parents' death. After that first day, that first night, it was just possible that she had not intentionally touched Evan since.

After a few minutes, he lay down, settling Bunn into the curve of his body, and she lay down beside him, one arm across his shoulders protectively. Pandora jumped onto the bed, kneading gently at the mattress for a moment before snuggling down against her in the space behind her knees. Together they formed a warm center in the softly lit room—warm and safe. All Drew's muscles seemed to let go; she realized she had been braced, every fiber and cell, against the return of the cold. Somehow she was certain that into this room, for tonight at least, the cold would not come.

She thought of the letters under the mattress in her room. She couldn't wait for Will. She would show them to Aunt Jocelyn in the morning. *Whatever your secret is, Amalie Broderick,* she thought in the direction of the writing room, *it's time they knew.*

"Crazy!" Aunt Jocelyn said the next morning, gesturing with her coffee mug at the letters spread in front of her on the table, so that she sloshed coffee on one of them. Drew had left Evan asleep and brought them down as soon as she heard Aunt Jocelyn up and around. "Amalie used to talk about her 'crazy friend.' They'd known each other since childhood, and Amalie couldn't bring herself to break off the relationship. That's the kind of person she was—loyal and loving, even to someone who had clearly become emotionally unstable, maybe psychotic. This is all nonsense. It tells us more about Dorothy than about Amalie."

"Don't you see?" Drew said, her stomach churning. What if Aunt Jocelyn couldn't be persuaded? "Even a crazy person couldn't just come up with this stuff by herself. She knew the name of the school you were supposed to go to—"

"Everyone knew that," Aunt Jocelyn said. "Amalie wanted me to have the best chance she could give me to develop my art, to make something of whatever talent she must have seen in me. For all the good it would have done."

"Then what about Evan?" Drew asked. "She must have tried to send him away, too, only your father wouldn't let her."

Jocelyn dismissed this. "I never heard anything about a boarding school for Evan."

"Maybe your father didn't like the idea from the beginning. Evan was just a little boy. Maybe your father just said no the minute Amalie suggested it. So you wouldn't have known."

Jocelyn shook her head. "No. Amalie loved Evan, especially Evan. She read to him, cuddled him, took him on long nature walks. There was nothing too good for Evan."

"'Bad enough you're going to have that little brat to deal with,'" Drew quoted from the April letter.

"Enough!" Jocelyn slammed her hand down on the table. "Those are Dorothy's words, not Amalie's. I knew Amalie. I lived in this house with her for more than a year. She was the most beautiful, the most loving— She was the best thing that ever happened to Father. To any of us. She brought life and light back into this sad, dark house!"

"Dorothy mentions a journal," Drew said.

"Amalie kept only one journal, her poetry journal. The one in the case at the library. I never knew of any other. No one ever knew of any other!"

"Maybe she did what Dorothy told her to do. Maybe she burned it."

There was a long silence. "I don't know what to tell you," Aunt Jocelyn said at last. "Maybe this whole thing won't work out, after all."

Drew's stomach did flip-flops. "What do you mean?"

"I hoped we could start fresh. A new generation. New relationships. I thought that this was a chance to build a family all over again. Perhaps it's a story that will never die." Jocelyn sighed. "Douglas tore what was left of this family apart, making those wild accusations about Amalie. Talking about finding that journal. There was already so much pain, and on top of it that last horrible scene. Father yelling, Douglas storming out. I thought I could handle this. I thought I could put the old hurt away and begin again. But you're Douglas's children. I would never have guessed it could be so clear. As if suspicion and doubt could be transmitted in the genes."

It was more than that, Drew thought. More than suspicion and doubt. And it didn't come from her genes.

"Your father left for college before Amalie came. He never really knew her. Never understood the difference she made."

Drew dabbed at the coffee-stained letter with a napkin. She kept hearing again what Aunt Jocelyn had said—that maybe this wouldn't work out, after all. Did that mean she and Evan might have to leave Rose Hill? That family and home were going to disappear again?

But she could not take back what she had said, could not stop thinking what she thought. Because she had seen Amalie, felt her hatred. Maybe it was because her father *hadn't* lived here with Amalie that he hadn't been fooled. And that was why she and Evan had never known about Rose Hill. Because no one could be welcome at Rose Hill who could not worship Amalie.

Tonight would be another night. Would Amalie come again? Would she come to gloat that she would always win? Her triumph would be that Drew and Evan would leave Rose Hill, and Amalie would stay. Amalie, dead now, needing nothing, would keep her home and loving family. Drew and Evan, who needed them desperately, would not.

No, Amalie, Drew thought as hard as she could, trying to direct the force of the thought upward. *You haven't won yet.*

CHAPTER
EIGHTEEN

WILL AND DREW sat on upturned crates in the greenhouse that afternoon when Will had finished his work. She had told him everything. She waited now, staring at the patterns the sun made on the floor while he read the letters from Dorothy. When he was done, he shook his head. "How could anybody who looked like Amalie be what these letters say?"

Drew shrugged. "You know the old saying, Beauty is as beauty does."

"Yeah, yeah. And beauty is only skin-deep, I know." He sighed. "I like the original Amalie a lot better than this one. Still, I don't see how anyone could quite buy that version after reading these letters. Your aunt doesn't actually know this Dorothy, does she? I mean, all she has to go on is what Amalie told her—about Dorothy being crazy. If someone wrote me letters like this, I'd want people to think she was crazy—in case they ever saw the letters."

Drew nodded. "Aunt Jocelyn just can't seem to bring herself to think Amalie might have been anything other than what everybody always thought—a sort of perfect person."

Will turned the letters over and over in his hands. "Whatever Amalie wrote to Dorothy, it wasn't the sort of thing a perfect person would write."

"I've been thinking," Drew said, "about Amalie bringing Evan the rabbit and singing to him. Do you think Amalie had two sides? Like a split personality? I saw the look in her eyes, and I know how scared I was of her. But maybe she isn't all bad. Just the way she wasn't all good. Maybe the way she is with me is her dark side, sort of, and the way she is with Evan is her light side. Aunt Jocelyn has two sides, too. She doesn't go in for a lot of hugging, but she's mostly warm and kind and even funny. And then, all of a sudden, she'll close off and be just hard and ferocious." Drew felt her eyes fill with tears as she remembered her aunt's words. "She says she doesn't know if it'll work out for Evan and me to stay here."

"What?" Will said. "But where would you go?"

"I don't know. I don't know." Her throat seemed to close off and it was a moment before she could speak again. "Maybe Amalie was—is—like that, too, with two sides. Could everybody be that wrong about her? People aren't all one thing. Nobody is." Drew had been thinking about how she'd treated Evan, how she'd almost ignored him for the last eight months. "I'm not."

Will folded up the letters carefully before he answered. "But even if you aren't all one thing, you aren't complete opposites. You don't go from being the most generous, loving person on the face of the earth to being a gold digger trying to get your new husband's kids shipped off to boarding school so they won't be under your feet all the time. Why did your aunt say she wasn't sure it would work out for you to stay here? Just because of Amalie?"

Drew nodded and blinked back tears. "It was

just because of Amalie that my father had to leave," she said when she could trust her voice. "Anyway, I don't know if I can live here with Amalie here, too, hating me. It's too scary. I would never be able to sleep. I can't even go up the front stairs anymore because I feel her behind me in the writing room."

"Then we've got to get rid of her, that's all. What about this journal Dorothy talks about? Do you think Amalie burned it, like she said?"

"No. Aunt Jocelyn said that letter didn't get here till after Amalie was dead. So even if she would have done what Dorothy said, she never had a chance. Nobody ever found the journal, though. My dad read the letters. He was the one who opened the last one. And he looked for the journal, too. That's why he left Rose Hill and never came back. Because he went to Grandfather about the letters. And Grandfather kicked him out—out of the house and out of the family. He wouldn't hear anything bad about Amalie, not even from his own son. Aunt Jocelyn thought the letters had been thrown away, but Dad had packed up Amalie's things, and he must have left them where he did on purpose—for someone to find someday."

"You're sure he didn't find the journal?"

"I'm sure. Aunt Jocelyn says there wasn't one."

"If Amalie kept it a secret, Jocelyn wouldn't have known. Dorothy knew, because Dorothy knew Amalie—really knew her. That journal is somewhere in the house, I'll make you a bet. We've got to find it. Whatever's in it would be in Amalie's own handwriting, and your aunt would have to believe."

"I don't see how we can find it if Dad couldn't."

"You want to stay here, don't you?"

Drew looked up at the broken and white-washed panes over her head and through them to the clear blue of the late-afternoon sky. "Yes."

"Then we have to get rid of Amalie. And I have a feeling that if we find that journal, one way or another, that's what we'll do. It's you or her, and I'm betting on you."

"You think we can beat her?"

Will grinned and nodded. "I told you before. Where there's a Will, there's a way."

Will's way began in the writing room. They waited until Jocelyn took her father's dinner tray in to him and then, while Evan was setting the table in the kitchen, slipped quietly up the back stairs. "I don't know if I can go in there again," Drew whispered when they reached the writing room door. "Anyway, why here? It could be anywhere in the house."

"This is *her* room. She wouldn't have trusted it anywhere else."

"What if she comes?"

"If she comes, you run. Simple. What can she do to you?"

"That's just it. I don't know."

"Nothing. Ghosts can't actually do anything except scare you. And then you do stuff to yourself."

Drew shuddered, remembering last night's headlong run down the stairs. "That could be enough."

"Shh. Come on." The door opened easily and they were inside. "Bookshelves first. You take that side, I'll take this side."

The air in the room was still and not cold. No smell except the slight hint of mildew and dust. Drew opened the doors on the glass-fronted bookcase and began reading the spines of the books. They were collections of poetry, mostly. Browning, Dickinson, Tennyson, Teasdale, Keats,

Shelley. Most of them were leather-bound and lettered in gold.

"Check the insides of any big ones," Will whispered. "If she was clever enough, she might have hidden her journal inside a book—cut out the pages, you know."

So Drew began opening any book that looked large enough to conceal even a small notebook. But all she found were dusty pages, some with notes in the margins, in Amalie's handwriting. When she'd checked every single book in the bookcase, she did her best to check behind it, between the back and the wall. But the shelf was too heavy to move even a couple of inches.

"Feel underneath, not just on the floor but up against the bottom of the shelf. She might have figured out a way to keep it up out of sight."

They found nothing in the bookshelves. While Drew began checking the desk, Will looked under the rug and felt for loose boards in the floor. After she'd looked under the velvet chair and felt to see whether something could be concealed in the cushions, Drew sat down. She was running her hand around the inside of the desk drawer when she felt the first chill. "Will," she said. "Will!"

He looked up from where he was crouched, near the door. "What? Did you find something?"

"C-c-cold," she stammered. "Do you smell—"

"Roses. I smell it all right." He dropped the rug back in place and hurried over. "It's colder over here. Do you suppose we're getting close? Is that it, Amalie? Are we getting close? Is it somewhere in your old desk?"

"There's nothing here," Drew said. "Unless the desk comes completely apart, I've looked everywhere. Let's go!"

"Wait by the door," Will said. "I'll give it one last look."

As Drew waited, her teeth beginning to chatter, more from nerves than from the cold, Will took the drawer completely out to check for a false bottom. "No luck," he said.

He was just starting to put the drawer back when the door to the writing room burst open and Aunt Jocelyn came in, her eyes blazing. Drew cowered back against the wall and Will stood up so fast, he dropped the drawer. Paper and paper clips scattered and the green marbleized pen rolled across the floor.

"What are you doing in here?" she demanded. "Who gave you permission?"

"We were looking for the journal," Will said, straightening his back and looking her in the eye.

"There was no journal!" Jocelyn said, her voice thick with anger. "I told you that, Drew! How dare you bring a stranger in here—"

Drew heard the echo of her grandfather's voice, calling Dr. Merriam a stranger. "Will isn't a stranger," she said. "He's a friend. We think there was a journal. Dad thought so, too. If there is, it's important to find it."

Evan appeared in the hallway behind Jocelyn, his eyes wide with questions, Pandora at his side.

For a moment, Aunt Jocelyn just stood there, her hands on her hips, gazing down at the jumble on the floor. Drew watched her, waiting for her answer, hardly daring to breathe. Her aunt's nostrils twitched and she rubbed a hand over her face as if trying to wipe something away. "Put that back the way it was," she said then. "Exactly the way it was. And then"—she turned on Will—"you will leave. And from now on, you stay *outside,* where your work is. You are not to come into this house again. Do you understand?"

Will nodded. "I'll go. But there is a journal, and someone needs to find it."

Aunt Jocelyn turned on her heel and started out, nearly colliding with Evan in the hall. Pandora, dodging feet, scurried into the room. The cat took a step toward Will and then froze. She arched her back, puffed her tail, and began to yowl.

CHAPTER
NINETEEN

DREW LAY ON her stomach on her bed, exhausted from crying, her cheek against her damp pillow. She had been wrong, of course. It wasn't true that once she started crying she would cry forever. Eventually, it had to stop. Not because there was no more pain—there was enough of that, she was sure, to last a lifetime and beyond—but because there was no more energy.

She felt like a landscape after a terrible storm, wet, still, empty, everything flattened. After this, Aunt Jocelyn was sure to send them back to the Tildens. She had been so angry.

If she and Evan had to leave Rose Hill, the

loss would be complete—for both of them. In the explosion, they had lost their parents and their present. Now they would lose their past, their history. They had only just found it and now it would be gone.

If the Tildens were not in Europe, Drew felt certain, Aunt Jocelyn would send them away immediately.

She turned over and lay for a few minutes looking at Aunt Jocelyn's watercolors. The Broderick curse, she thought. Hopes shattered, beginnings smashed, potential lost. She had begun to feel something inside her opening up, just the first stirrings. Some of it had been because of Aunt Jocelyn. The way she had seemed to accept them so easily, slipping them into her life as if they had been away only a while and had returned, to fill their old places.

Some of it had been Will. Drew thought of Will as she'd first seen him—could it be only weeks ago?—skidding to a stop on his old bike, his tanned arms and legs gangly in cutoffs and T-shirt, his hair flopping into his eyes.

And some of it had been Rose Hill—the lawns and trees, the hills and meadows, and the beauty of the house. It had felt so *meant,* so right, as if whatever had stolen her first life—God, fate, the universe—had given her this one, not to take its place but to let her continue, let her begin to live again. And now whatever had begun opening had closed.

There had been no one to blame for the first incomprehensible loss. Gas leak, the police had said, act of God. But this was Amalie's fault. Drew sat up and pushed her damp hair out of her face. Amalie's fault. No matter what she had done for Evan, it was Amalie who was driving them away.

"I won't give up," she whispered into the warm air around her. "Daddy did. But I won't. I'll find your journal, Amalie, I promise you that."

When Drew opened her eyes, it was black dark. She must have fallen asleep without turning on a light, without even pulling up the quilt. But she didn't need a light to know that Amalie was in the room. The scent of roses wrapped itself with the cold around her. She gagged and gasped for breath. "You can't hurt me," she managed to say. "Will said you can't."

But the crack in her voice gave her away even to herself. It was something about the cold that brought fear with it, no matter how she fought against it. Already, she was shaking all over. She became aware of a soft film of moonlight, graying the darkness. She could make out no more than a deeper darkness, a shadow's shadow. But it was coming closer, sending a chill ahead of it like waves, a chill and a sense of menace.

Stay where you are, she told herself—she can't hurt you. But she felt herself moving as if she were a puppet, being operated by someone else, someone whose will had nothing to do with her own. She was sitting up, her feet swinging over the side of the bed, the urge to run swelling inside her like a balloon. The waves of cold were beating against her now as the darkness closed in, and she was on her feet, tearing open the door. She managed to turn on the hall light, and then she was on the stairs, flying down them, barely feeling the rug beneath her feet as she went.

She crashed into the front door and tried to open it. Locked. She twisted the dead bolt. Stuck. This has happened before, she realized with terrible clarity. She beat on the door with her fists, then turned, to see Amalie drifting, almost sailing down the long stairs, her dress fluttering, the look of hatred like a blue flame burning through the cold. Drew turned back to the door and wrenched the dead bolt with both hands. It gave at last and the door was open.

She was through it and down the stone steps, onto the drive. She was aware of stones tearing at her bare feet, but she ran on, past the carriage house, the greenhouse, aware of nothing but the desperate need to get away from the form she knew without looking pursued her, closing the space between them. She ran and ran, her breath a tearing, burning sensation in her chest. Fear grew with every step until there was nothing but the fear, driving her forward into the darkness.

"Drew! DREW!"

The sound of her name shattered the night and brought her to a sudden skidding stop. She took a deep, ragged breath, feeling consciousness slam into her body like a stretched rubber band snapping back. The smell of mud and rot rose around her and she found herself up to her ankles in mud, surrounded by the dim shapes of cattails. Ahead, past the dark scum of duckweed, lay the soft silver shine of the pond. She looked over her shoulder, straining to feel as much as to see the shape that had pursued her. Nothing but the empty night and a few fireflies winking their yellow lights like sparks in the darkness. And then she saw Evan, a small pale form in the moonlight, standing in the ruts of the old road, the rabbit dangling by an ear from one hand.

"Evan? Was that you?"

He moved and she could make out the nod, but he did not speak again.

She tried to turn and found that she could not pull her feet free. The stench of the muck nearly overwhelmed her as she tried, and her dream rose up again, the heaviness of her legs, the sticky something dragging at her feet. Wishing she had something to hold on to, she tried again, but she could not pull free. As she tugged at one foot, her weight on the other seemed to sink that one even farther. Finally, holding her breath against the smell, she threw herself down into the muck. On hands and knees, using cattails to pull herself forward, she dragged herself toward Evan.

At last, she felt firm ground beneath her and managed to scramble onto the old road, next to Evan. She sat for a moment, shuddering against the smell and feel of the slime that coated her body, plastering her pajamas against her skin. When she had caught her breath, she reached out and touched Evan's hand.

"You saved my life. Another minute and I would have been too far to get back."

Evan nodded.

"It was your voice I heard. You can talk."

He opened his mouth, his whole face straining, but no sound came. Tears left silver tracks down his cheeks.

"Never mind," she said. "You did it—when you had to. It'll come."

She stood then and took his free hand. It was warm in hers, and small. She could not remember a feeling more wonderful.

When they got close to the house, limping on scratched and bruised bare feet, Pandora came to greet them, meowing a welcome. She followed them to the greenhouse and leapt onto the table, staying well out of the way as Drew used the hose to wash Evan's feet. When that was done, Drew turned the water on herself, almost glad of the chill that washed the foul-smelling muck onto the broken concrete floor. At least this cold had a reason, an ordinary, real-life source. When she was passably clean, dripping but no longer smelling of muck, she turned off the hose. She squeezed as much water out of her pajamas as she could and took Evan's hand again. "Let's go," she whispered. Pandora stretched herself, jumped down, and followed them. They stopped for a moment in the doorway as Drew looked at the house, so calm and still and beautiful in the moonlight.

You haven't won yet, she thought toward the second floor, toward the closed writing room.

"Is Aunt Jocelyn up, do you think?" she asked Evan.

He shook his head.

"Okay, then. Be very, very quiet. We'll go up the back way and I'll stay in your room tonight." She didn't even pretend to herself that this was for his sake.

CHAPTER
TWENTY

THEY CREPT AS quietly as they could past Jocelyn's room and their grandfather's. Upstairs, the light was still on. The hall was empty—quiet, hot. No hint of cold or the scent of roses.

She took Evan into his room and left him on the bed, propped against his pillows, with Pandora next to him. Then she went back to her own room and changed into a clean nightgown. She gathered up Lulu and the quilt from her bed.

She peeked into the hall before scurrying back across. Still empty. Leaving the light on behind her, she carefully closed Evan's door, satisfied to hear the reassuring click that latched it. Drew knew that no door could keep Amalie out if she wanted to come in, but this was Evan's room, and she still had a feeling that it was safe. As she had before, she felt oddly comforted just being here, under the watching eyes of the lions and tigers, in the glow of the elephant lamp.

Drew sat on the edge of the bed. Evan's hair was tousled and his cheeks smudged from rubbing away tears. She set Lulu next to Bunn, took both of Evan's hands in hers, and peered intently into his eyes. "You called my name out there."

He sniffed and nodded, then opened his mouth as if to speak, frowned, and closed it again.

"Come on, Evan. You did it before. You can do it again."

He closed his eyes, squeezing them very tightly, as if concentrating. At last, slowly and haltingly, he began to speak, his voice hoarse and strained. "I—I h-had to. He t-told me I had to or something awful w-w-would happen to you. He tr-tried, but you c-c-couldn't hear him."

Drew was listening so hard to the unaccustomed sound of her brother's voice that she didn't at first take in what he had said. Then it registered. "Who? Who tried?"

Evan opened his eyes. He scanned the room

quickly and then focused on the rocking chair. "Evan."

Drew sat very still, trying to take in the meaning of what he had said. "Who?"

"Evan. The first Evan. Daddy's brother."

Drew dropped her brother's hands and pulled the quilt more tightly around her shoulders. "You mean you've seen the first Evan? He's talked to you?"

Evan nodded solemnly. "He's a ghost. He says he didn't know it at first. But then nobody could see him. Nobody could hear him. He wanted to tell everybody what happened. But he couldn't make them know he was there. So he knew he was a ghost." Evan's mouth drooped. "He was very sad and very lonely for a long, long time. Till I came."

Drew thought about a ghost child waiting alone in this room for more than thirty years for someone to listen to his story. "When did you first see him?"

"The night we came. He was sitting on the bed when I came back from brushing my teeth. He scared me, because I didn't know there was anyone else here. I think I scared him, too. At first, he couldn't believe I could see him. I—I tried to talk to him, but I couldn't. And then it didn't matter. He could understand even if I couldn't talk. So it was all right. And we found out we were both named Evan, and he said maybe that's why I could see him."

Suddenly, Drew understood the lure of this room, the hours Evan had spent alone here. "So the two of you have been playing together in here?"

Evan nodded. "He comes outside sometimes, too. We go to the carriage house. It was his favorite place—when he was alive." Evan reached down and petted Pandora, who turned up her chin to be rubbed and began purring. "He likes Pandora. He never had a cat."

Drew was thinking as fast as she could, piecing together the bits of the puzzle. It wasn't that Amalie had been different for Evan. It hadn't been Amalie at all. "Does Evan sing to you sometimes?" she asked.

Evan nodded. "He taught me his favorite song, and I would do it with him and he said it was as good as singing it, even if I couldn't make sounds anybody else could hear. It was sort of like we were the only people in the whole world who could hear each other. Except people could see me. He said maybe I was half a ghost."

Drew felt her eyes fill suddenly. She grabbed him and hugged him hard. "You aren't even a little bit of a ghost. You're whole and alive and real. And I can hear you talking."

Evan grinned. "So can I."

"Do you know who that woman was who chased me tonight?"

"She's a ghost, too." Evan's voice was low. "But not nice like Evan. He says we have to be very careful of her. She's in the story he wanted to tell."

"What about her?"

Evan stared at his hands, clasping and unclasping them. "She drowned him, Drew. In that place you were tonight. That's why he said I had to make you hear, because you were running toward that place, that end of the pond where Aunt Jocelyn said we shouldn't ever go. She drowned him on purpose, he says, and she probably wanted you to drown, too." Evan paused for a moment and then went on. "She made a mistake back then about the pond. That's how come she's a ghost. Because after she drowned him, she couldn't get out again."

Drew remembered the story the way Mrs.

Connelly had told it. Amalie on her way to visit the sick friend. Flat tire. The "providence" that she just happened to be on the back road when Evan, out looking for foxes, fell into the pond. Amalie sacrificing her life trying to save her beloved stepson. All of it a lie. Had it all been planned? Had she told Dorothy that plan in a letter—or hinted at it?

"That's a pretty terrible story," she said.

Evan nodded. "She was a terrible person. Evan wants people—especially Aunt Jocelyn—to know what Amalie did. When she knows, he can quit being a ghost."

"Quit? How can he quit?"

Drew watched Evan's face lighten, as if the gloom that had for so long shadowed his features was lifting in front of her eyes. "He can go," Evan said quietly. "He says there's a place all full of light where he can go when he's done what he's been waiting to do. Where he won't be a ghost anymore."

"A place all full of light," Drew repeated. Heaven? "How does he know about this place?"

"He saw it. And when he goes there, he'll be real again, not like this, not where nobody can see him or hear him except me."

Drew patted Evan's hand. "You tell Evan next time you see him that I've heard him. I've heard him singing."

"Tell him yourself," Evan said.

Drew caught her breath. "How? You don't mean he's here."

Evan nodded and pointed to the rocking chair. She could see nothing except the empty chair. With a start, she saw that it was rocking ever so slightly. "Tell him," Evan said.

"I heard you singing," she said. "I'm sorry I can't see you. And I didn't hear you very well. But I knew somebody was in here with Evan."

"He's glad," Evan said, and she turned back to him.

"Evan, would you ask him a question for me? And listen very carefully to his answer so you can tell me what he says?" Evan nodded. "Ask him if he knows about a book Amalie used to write in. A secret book—a journal—she didn't let anyone see."

The room was quiet, but Evan was looking with focused attention at the rocking chair, which had stopped rocking. Drew realized that the two Evans were communicating without her hearing anything at all.

"Yes. He knows about the book. She didn't think anybody ever saw it, but he did. She used to hide it."

Drew crossed her fingers before asking the next question. Everything depended on the answer. "Does he know where it is?"

Again the silence, a curious silence that felt somehow alive. And then the simple and wonderful answer: "Yes."

"Where?"

"It's in her room, but no one can get it."

That couldn't be. If it was hidden in the writing room, they'd find it no matter what. "Why not?"

Pandora rolled over on her back and crooked a paw across her nose, apparently no more able to sense the communication that was going on in the room than Drew was.

"She guards it," came the answer. "She won't let anyone get near. And she's dangerous."

Drew sighed. The rest of the puzzle pieces fell into place. Dorothy must have been right. However much of her plan Amalie had written to Dorothy, she must have put all of it into her journal. She had died without destroying the journal, so she had come back to make sure it stayed forever hidden. The position and reputation she had built had been everything to her when she was alive; in death, it must be all that was left. Drew wondered whether Amalie had ever cared about Gilbert Broderick, the old man who lay downstairs now, near death himself, a victim of three decades of inconsolable grief. Because of his love, she thought, for a phantom. A fake.

"We have to get it," she told Evan now. "Tell him we have to get it."

"The only way would be to get her away from the hiding place. But she never leaves."

Never leaves, Drew thought. But she does. She'd gone halfway down the stairs last night. And tonight, chasing Drew, she'd gone almost all the way to the pond.

"We'll think of something," Drew said. "Tomorrow, we'll talk to Will." She grinned at Evan and then at the rocking chair, which had begun moving again. "You know what he says. Where there's a Will..."

Drew went to sleep that night, next to Evan, feeling light, safe, hopeful. And sometime in the night, or maybe only in a dream, she heard again the light voice singing.

CHAPTER
TWENTY-ONE

"DREW! DREW, COME down here. Evan, you too." Aunt Jocelyn's voice was like flint on steel. "Immediately!"

Drew, having just gone to her room to get dressed, hastily pulled a T-shirt over her head and hurried down the hall toward the back steps. It can't be much past seven, she thought as she went. What could Aunt Jocelyn be upset about? She heard Evan's door open as he came behind her.

At the top of the steps, she saw. The muddy trail they had left last night was perfectly clear—up the center of the stairs. Two sets of bare feet and Pandora's paw tracks winding in and out.

"What is the meaning of this mess?" her aunt asked.

Drew thought fast. She dared not mention Amalie, not until they found the journal and had proof of what Evan one had told them. She hoped Evan, now that he could talk, wouldn't try to explain. "We couldn't sleep last night. So we went out for a walk. I didn't realize we'd left such a mess. I'll clean it up."

Jocelyn's frown deepened. "You went for a walk? In the middle of the night?" But before there was time for an answer, the bell rang from Grandfather's room—once, twice, three times. Aunt Jocelyn glanced toward his closed door and back at them. "I've been up since before dawn," she said. "Father's in a bad way. I can't handle any more problems today!"

"You won't have to," Drew assured her. "We'll get this cleaned up. You look after Grandfather and we'll take care of ourselves. You don't have to think about us at all today. It's all right."

Pandora appeared suddenly and bounded down the stairs. She rubbed against Jocelyn's legs, meowing lightly.

Jocelyn's expression softened for a moment

and she reached to rub the cat's ears. The bell rang again, followed by a weak, raspy voice. "Jocelyn, come!"

She turned and hurried to his room.

"I'm glad you didn't mention Amalie," Drew said to Evan when the door had closed. "No one is going to believe us without the journal."

Evan's voice this morning was rough again. "I—w-was scared to talk. She looked so m-mad."

"Let's just stay out of her way today. Will should be here in a little while. He's supposed to cut the grass. Meantime, let's find some rags and get this cleaned up."

While Drew and Evan were eating cereal a little while later, Aunt Jocelyn called Dr. Merriam on the kitchen phone. The conversation was brief. When she hung up, she turned to them, her face more strained and drawn than Drew had ever seen it. "They're sending a nurse in a few hours to give Father a transfusion," she said. "I'd appreciate it if the two of you would stay out from underfoot."

Underfoot. It was the expression Dorothy had used to Amalie about Jocelyn, Drew remembered. She nodded.

Pandora was batting her spool around the

kitchen floor, pouncing as it ricocheted off the baseboards. Jocelyn stood for a moment, watching. Then she went to the sink to wash her hands. "And keep the cat with you," she said. "There will be a lot of coming and going, and I don't want her to get into Father's room."

"Incredible!" Will said in the greenhouse later. He had been sharpening a hoe as he listened to their story.

"We have to find the journal," Drew said.

Will leaned the hoe against the plant table. He shoved his hair out of his eyes and looked at Evan. "Amalie's never come after you, has she?"

Evan, sitting on the floor, moving a twig for Pandora to chase, shook his head. Then, as if remembering suddenly that he could, he spoke. "The other Evan thinks she doesn't care about me because I never went to the writing room."

Will nodded. "She doesn't consider you a threat."

"That's changed, though," Drew said. "He knows the whole story. Now that he can talk, he's as much of a threat to her as I am."

"Oh, right. Well...so much for my plan. I thought we could send Evan into the writing room with Evan—I mean with Evan one—and Evan one could show him where the journal is."

Drew shook her head. "No way. Nobody should go into that room while she's there. Evan one says she'll guard that journal from anyone. And she's dangerous." She shuddered, remembering the sudden moment of waking, to find herself ankle-deep in swamp. "She could have killed me last night."

"I have an idea," Evan said. He put down the twig and gathered Pandora into his lap, rubbing his cheek against the top of her head. "Evan and I talked about it."

"This is too much," Will said.

Drew nodded. "Go ahead, Evan. What's the idea?"

"We get her to chase me—"

"Oh, no. No way."

"Let him finish," Will said.

"Tonight, when Aunt Jocelyn and Grandfather are asleep, I get up and pretend I'm going into the writing room. If Amalie comes after me"—he looked up at Drew—"I do what you did last night. I run downstairs and out the front door. As soon as she follows me, you and Evan can go into the writing room and get the journal."

"But I can't see him! Or hear him."

"That doesn't matter. He'll be able to show you."

"Why doesn't he just tell you where it is?" Will asked.

"It wouldn't matter," Drew reminded him. "Somebody would still have to be able to get in when she wasn't there to get it." She thought of the sense of warmth and comfort in Evan's room. "Anyway, I'd rather have him with me than go in there by myself."

"Okay. Right."

Drew frowned then and shook her head. "It won't work anyway."

"Why not?" Evan asked.

"Because I can't let you play bait. You don't know what she's like. I couldn't help myself last night. I just ran. I didn't know where I was going or how long I'd been running or anything. I just had to run. It was awful."

There was a long silence. Drew felt the sun beating against the back of her neck through a broken pane in the whitewashed glass above.

"What if I was with him?" Will asked. "I could tell Mom I was spending the night with a friend, and you could sneak me in to Evan's room. Then I could stay with him the whole time."

"What good would that do? She'd just get both of you."

Will shook his head. "Not me. Remember what I said about ghosts not being able to hurt you unless you hurt yourself? It's the fear that does it. And I'm not that scared of Amalie. All I'd have to do is think what a bad poet she was, and that would keep her from getting to me. I could memorize one of the really schmaltzy poems and say it out loud if I start to get scared. What do you think?"

Drew looked into Will's eyes. Could he really do it?

He looked right back at her, his eyes clear and eager, and grinned, his braces sparkling in the sun. "Where there's..."

"Yeah, yeah." She grinned back. "Okay, but we've got to make sure everything goes exactly right. I don't want Evan to have to face Amalie alone. And whatever you do, don't head for the pond."

"We'll get it right," Will assured her.

CHAPTER

TWENTY-TWO

BUT IT ISN'T all that easy to get it right, Drew thought a little after one in the morning as she stood poised at the top of the front stairs, flashlight in hand, while Aunt Jocelyn paced back and forth in the hall beneath her. They had planned that after Aunt Jocelyn went to bed, Drew would sneak down and let Will in the front door so that he could stay with Evan in his room. Drew had made sure, when she went up for the night, that the front door was unlocked. She'd left a small lamp burning in the living room so that when Evan and Will got to the bottom of the stairs, with Amalie after them, they wouldn't have any trouble getting the door open. But Aunt Jocelyn had not gone to bed.

Grandfather's call bell had rung every couple of hours, even after the nurse had left, having assured them that the transfusion would do wonders for him. Aunt Jocelyn had barely taken time to eat the sandwich Drew had made her for dinner. "I don't dare sleep," she'd said later, "for fear he'll get worse in the night and be too weak to call me. If I sit in that room with him, I just know I'll fall asleep."

And so she was pacing, keeping herself awake to answer her father's slightest call, checking in on him every so often and then going back to her vigil in the hall.

There was no sign of any movement in the writing room, no chill to the air, no smell of roses. But Drew had all she could do not to run back to her room and slam the door. The light coming up the stairwell only served to make the darkness worse, throwing shadows against the walls. Drew hoped Will was still waiting outside. Unless they could set the whole thing up again tomorrow night, they needed to go ahead with the plan tonight. Surely Aunt Jocelyn wouldn't pace the hall till morning.

Just as she thought this, Drew heard the sound of a door being opened downstairs. Carefully, she crept down a couple of steps and listened. It was Grandfather's door, she thought. Aunt Jocelyn must be checking again. She waited, holding her breath. No sound. And still no sound. After what she judged to be five minutes, Drew relaxed. Her aunt must have decided to settle in the chair by her father's bedside. Maybe she had just gotten too tired to keep pacing. Drew waited another minute, just to be sure.

She had just started downstairs to let Will in when she heard Evan's door open above her. No, she thought, don't come out yet! But it was too late. He stopped for a moment at the head of the stairs, and she gestured for him to go back. She didn't dare say anything for fear of alerting Aunt Jocelyn.

But he didn't go back. He went instead toward the front of the house. She started back up to try to catch him, but already the upstairs hall was cold, the scent of roses growing.

She stood for a second watching Evan's thin back in short pale blue pajamas (he'd worn his sneakers, as she'd told him to) move closer to the writing room door. He's being braver, she thought, than I could be. The cold seemed to push her backward, toward Evan's room, where Evan one was supposed to be waiting for her. There's still time, she thought, to yell at Evan, to stop the whole thing. But then, in the pale light coming from downstairs, she saw the misty form swirling in front of the writing room door. As she watched, barely breathing, Amalie took on solidity and shape. The cascade of blond hair, the soft flowery dress, the beautiful face. And the eyes, blue flames focused on Evan. The shape began to move.

Run! she thought at Evan as she stepped back into the shadows of the doorway to his room. As if he'd heard her, he turned and headed for the stairs. The shape of Amalie came after him, toward Drew, so it was all Drew could do to stay where she was, gripping the barrel of her flashlight until her fingers went numb. The waves of cold washed over her, and just as she felt her mind giving in to the fear, her stomach churning her dinner into her throat, she felt a warmth at her elbow, a space where the cold seemed to be turned back.

Evan one, she thought, and immediately she was able to swallow, to calm her stomach and

begin thinking clearly again. Evan had reached
the front door now and was struggling with the
handle. Drew could see him past—through—the
figure of Amalie as it swept down toward him.
Had Aunt Jocelyn locked the door again? But
then the door was opening and Drew saw Will
rising from the front steps, his face white in the
light spilling from the hall. She watched as he
grabbed Evan's hand and the two began to move
quickly, but not running, across the drive and
into the darkness.

The sense of warmth at her side reminded
Drew that she had a vital part in this plan. She
took two quick breaths, flicked on her flashlight,
and hurried to the writing room. The door
opened easily and she was inside. "Are you here,
Evan?" she asked. "How are you going to show
me?"

She swept the flashlight around the room.
Everything was as it had always been. No place
she could see where a journal could possibly be
that they hadn't already looked. Suddenly, the
shade at the window flipped up, making a sharp
slapping sound that frightened her so badly, she
nearly dropped her light. When she recovered,
she could see the silver disk of the nearly full

moon riding high in the darkness outside. There was a sharp knocking sound near the window. After a second, it was repeated.

She hurried over, her light playing on the window, the woodwork around it, the sill. Nothing. The knock sounded again. It was coming from the right side of the window frame. She leaned over the desk and felt the woodwork. The window was deeply set, the woodwork unusually wide. As she felt the edges of the painted surface, it moved. She shone the light there and saw that what she had thought was woodwork was really a sort of hinged door. She opened it. Behind the door was a shutter, folded into the space behind, covered with dust and cobwebs. Nothing else.

"It isn't there—," she started to say, when the shutter door slammed shut, nearly catching her hand, and the knock sounded, louder. "It isn't there!" she repeated. Then she noticed that there was another shutter door immediately above— one shutter for the lower panes of the window, one for the upper. She reached up and pried the upper door open. Inside was another space, another shutter, and, in the light of the flashlight, a dusty leather-bound volume. The journal!

She pulled it out and dropped it onto the desk, shining the flashlight on the now-familiar handwriting. It was Amalie's, all right. She flipped pages until she found the last few that had been written. Quickly, she scanned the pages. And it was there. Under the heading "August 6, 1961," Amalie had begun construct-ing her plan.

Drew closed the book, sneezing as dust rose around her, and clutched it to her chest. Now all they had to do—

The scream came from outside. It was Evan. There was no mistaking it. Drew ran from the writing room, flashlight in one hand, journal in the other. As she reached the top of the stairs, she saw Pandora puffed to nearly twice her normal size, standing in the open doorway, looking out into the night. As Evan, somewhere out there, screamed again, Pandora began to yowl.

CHAPTER

TWENTY-THREE

DREW FLUNG HERSELF down the stairs, past Aunt Jocelyn, who had come hurrying from her father's room, and out the door, nearly tripping on the cat, who continued to yowl.

The flashlight bounced crazily, sending its beam into the sky, across the trees, anywhere except on the ground ahead as Drew ran. But she barely needed the light. The moon was bright enough to cast shadows, and she knew exactly where she was going—down the back drive, to the old road. Amalie had done it again, driven Evan and Will to the pond. Even now, running as fast as her feet would carry her, Drew was afraid she might be too late. "No!" she gasped. "You can't have him, too!"

She came to the turning and followed the weed-grown ruts, slipping and sliding on the wet grass. As the cattails began to be visible ahead, a dark shape loomed so suddenly in the path ahead that she nearly fell over it.

"Something pushed me," it said. It was Will, trying to stand. "I felt it! My ankle—"

As she skidded to a stop, struggling to keep her balance so that she wouldn't end up with Will in the muddy road, Drew felt a sensation, as if something had brushed past her. She moved around Will and hurried forward.

She splashed in among the cattails, feeling the mud suck at her sneakers, and saw Evan, standing up to his knees in the muck, facing this way, moonlight bright on his hair and face. Moving slowly, inexorably toward him was the figure of Amalie, seeming almost to glow, gliding through cattails and over the surface of the swamp.

Evan strained to pull a foot free, taking a step backward, then another. "Stand still!" Drew screamed. "Don't go any farther!"

Still, Amalie moved forward. Still, Evan tried

to back away. He seemed almost at the point of toppling backward into the black water, when the figure of Amalie jolted, as if she'd been struck from behind, and turned. Her eyes, burning with fury, scanned the surface of the swamp, the mass of cattails. Drew thought she heard across the water a light, taunting laugh. Then Amalie's eyes focused on her.

Drew held up the journal and shone the flashlight on it. "It's too late!" she yelled. "We've got your journal. And we'll show it to everyone. Aunt Jocelyn and Grandfather and everyone in Riverton. They'll know what you did—what you really were! You might as well go now, Amalie Broderick, wherever it is you're supposed to go. Because you're dead. And now your name will be dead, too. The masquerade is over."

For a moment, Drew felt as if time had stopped, as if everything had stopped. There was no sound, no movement. Just the strange scene in the moonlit swamp, Evan and Amalie and herself, holding the journal above her head. And then, slowly, the form of Amalie Broderick began to swell, getting bigger and at the same time paler, less clearly visible, its edges softening and swirling until, like smoke above a campfire, it dwindled into a fine whorl of shimmery gray and vanished.

Drew thought she caught the sound of singing, little more than an echo moving over the surface of the pond. "I see the moon, the moon sees me..."

And then Evan was singing, too. "Down through the leaves of the old oak tree. I see the moon, the moon sees me. God bless the moon and God bless me."

Drew splashed forward to get to Evan and bring him back. "Don't go out there!" Will called. "Find a stick and hold it out to him."

Drew remembered how hard it had been to get back to solid ground. "Stay where you are," she called to Evan. He nodded.

Drew turned and saw Aunt Jocelyn standing next to Will, a huge flashlight dangling from her hand, its beam aimed at the base of a clump of cattails on the edge of the swamp. She was staring across the water, her mouth open, her head tilted to one side as if listening.

CHAPTER

TWENTY-FOUR

DREW AND AUNT Jocelyn found a branch long enough to reach to Evan, and he managed, with their help, to pull himself free of the muck. Then they helped Will back to the house, supporting his weight between them as he hopped on his good foot.

"What a mess," Aunt Jocelyn said when they'd settled Will in the kitchen on one chair, with his leg supported by another. They'd left their shoes by the back door, but Evan's had vanished in the marsh, so he stood with the mud running off his legs and feet onto the yellow tile.

"It'll wash off," he said.

Aunt Jocelyn had bent to check Will's ankle.

She stood up straight, her hand against her chest, and looked at Evan. "Say that again."

"It'll wash off."

She nodded. "Yes. I guess it will." She turned to Drew. "Sings and talks, too. I suppose we'll never have another peaceful moment. You two get yourselves upstairs and cleaned up and then come back here. I'll check on Father and deal with Will's ankle. Then I'll make some tea and you will provide some explanations. All of you!"

Later, while her tea cooled, Drew read the last pages of Amalie's journal out loud. Aunt Jocelyn sat very still, her tea, too, untouched, stroking Pandora, who was curled, purring loudly, in her lap. When the reading was done, Aunt Jocelyn sat for a long time, staring down at her fingers as they moved through the cat's white fur. Finally, she raised her head. Tears glistened on her cheeks. "It's almost more than I can take in, even hearing it in her own voice. Our Evan. How could Amalie—how could *anyone*—?

"She must have waited to leave that night until she was sure Evan had gone out looking for the foxes. The cold-bloodedness of it—jamming an ice pick into her tire and then heading for the pond—" She lifted her hand to run one finger around the edge of her teacup. "And I did just what she knew I would. Johnny and I." She closed her eyes and shook her head. "It worked exactly the way she'd planned, except she'd never been in the pond. She didn't know what it was like."

"You have to tell Grandfather," Drew said. "So he'll know it wasn't your fault."

Pandora's purring filled the silence before Jocelyn finally spoke. "Wasn't it?"

"Of course not!"

"If you'd kept your eye on Evan that night, she could have waited till you'd gone off to school and done it then," Will said.

"I suppose." Jocelyn rubbed behind Pandora's ears. "I can't quite take it in. My whole life—" She stopped. "I won't tell Father. Amalie was the great love of his life. He used to say she was a miracle. He's dying. I can't take Amalie away from him."

"He'll know," Evan said, his eyes solemn, "after."

"Perhaps. But not now. And not from me."

After a moment, Will spoke. "I guess we know for sure now that ghosts are real."

"And the place of light," Evan said. "That's real, too."

The place of light. Were Douglas and Marianne Broderick there? Drew wondered. As if he had heard her thought, Evan nodded at her.

And Drew felt something inside her open up—like a fist unclenching.

Suddenly, they heard a faint childish voice, singing, "I see the moon, the moon sees me. God bless the moon and God bless me."

Pandora stopped purring and raised her head, ears twitching.

"He used to sing that all the time," Jocelyn said, "all the time." Her eyes brimmed with tears, but she smiled. "It drove me crazy."

In the silence, Evan kept listening. "He says everything's all right. He's going now." Evan frowned. "I'll miss him."

"This time, I can say it," Jocelyn said. "Goodbye, Evan."

"He wants you to know he loves you."

"I love him, too."

They sat still, listening. But there was no more sound.

Drew looked from face to face around the kitchen table—her aunt, her brother, her friend. Evan grinned at her, his old elfish grin, and she grinned back. *We're home.*